The Earth in Peril

1

It was one of those stormy days in Mungongoh. Not the kind of storm you generally have on earth, however, for Mungongoh never had rain, cloudy weather or heavy winds. The storm was actually coming from inside the palace of king Awobua, the sovereign ruler of Mungongoh. He was engaged in what was supposed to be his favourite pastime, but seemed rather to be in the throes of some stressful situation as he howled wildly in pain and disappointment.

King Awobua was wearing an expensive *dalla* of black cloth with intricate red embroidery around the neckline, on the chest and back, and along the edges. The *dalla* was the customary dress of Mungongoh men; it could be more or less elaborate depending on the occasion. In his position as king of Mungongoh, Awobua always wore the best, produced by a master in this special design. Unlike kings on earth, he did not have a court. Neither did he have a troop of scheming and pompous courtiers, competing with each other for the favours of the king, while showing exaggerated and false loyalty, and reverence when ever they thought they had his attention. There was thus no flamboyant and flirtatious crowd in this special room where the king was sitting. King Awobua was a loner to some degree, preferring to concentrate on the large monitor in front of him and to watch scenes of every activity on earth that he could capture. The royal abode was the size of a handball pitch. The king was attended by dwarfs who catered to his personal needs and served him. His throne was a simple swivel chair upholstered in lionskin; the same material was used for the throw rugs he used as foot mats. The king spent all waking hours here and only moved into his bedroom next door to sleep. He ate and drank in this room and his solitary meals were served by timorous stewards, who escaped to the safety of the kitchen the moment the meal was served. He was a solidly built man and strong as an ox. His corresponding anger was unpredictable and mercifully not often directly felt by the people, since they were hardly ever in his presence. He had a normal appetite and drank in moderation in his lair. Apart from the king's private quarters, the palace also contained the offices of the chief minister and some senior officials.

King Awobua turned away angrily from the large screen on which he had been concentrating and buzzed for Mobuh, his most senior minister. The king had just been watching a victim of the Fire plague that he had sprayed on the earth rise to his feet and walk shakily. The chap was supposed to have been writhing in excruciating pain, after which he was expected to die horribly. Instead, he was getting up in defiance of the terrible Fire plague. The man staggered forward, retched and vomited, but still remained on his feet. He was moving towards a female who was lying prostrate and helpless. She stirred as he touched her and raised a feeble hand up for help.

The Fire plague had actually fallen on the earth like one of those sudden tsunamis in the Pacific. The earthlings, who had been going about their normal business oblivious of any looming danger, were not prepared for such a virulent killer. When the Fire plague struck with full force, nobody thought that rats could be linked to it. After all, the bubonic plague that swept through Europe hundreds of years ago had been tamed and mastered. When it persisted however, it was discovered that rats were the main form of transmission, but there was no ready solution to the spread

2

of this present pestilence. All attempts to corral it were unsuccessful as the virus kept mutating into something else. The Fire plague did not discriminate and swept away every human obstacle it came across. Paupers, sportsmen, doctors, ministers, presidents, no one was spared. The earth's population was actually disappearing. The religious had offered or participated in special prayers to rid the earth of the Fire plague. Quack witch doctors and fortune-tellers had made wild predictions and speculations in vain. Even palmisters and astrologers had sought to explain the root cause and trend of the Fire plague by interpreting signs in the positions of the stars and constellations. While the whole world was suffering, a few smart people were actually making money. Fake medicines and vaccines were sold and countless booklets on prevention of the Fire plague, printed.

However, as the Fire plague raged on, nobody could put a finger on the source of the pestilence. Many assumed it to be some form of divine punishment for the evil ways of the inhabitants of the earth. Others simply blamed it on the proliferation of rats, whose populations had carelessly been allowed to multiply unchecked. No one thought of the possibility that the virulent disease might be of extraterrestrial origin. From the king's observatory he could discern that a flaw was surfacing in this apparently wonderful attempt to rid the earth of humans. As the English say, *you cannot have your cake and eat it* and the king was now having a taste of this wise saying. The Fire plague was killing earthlings in their numbers but the fact that a few were already surviving from it was proof that many earthlings would survive.

King Awobua, who had been highly elated by the great strides of the Fire plague, was now beaten and downcast. He would have to come up with something else to wipe away humans from the surface of the earth and colonise it with his people. He shifted uncomfortably in is seat, cursed wildly, and brought down his right fist viciously on the head

3

of one of his dwarf attendants. The diminutive fellow howled in anguish as blood gushed out of his mouth and nostrils. King Awobua did not seem to notice the effect of his violence on the dwarf. It was his usual way of taking out his anger and this means of venting his frustration had often resulted in the deformation and even the death of some of the creatures. The citizens of Mungongoh planet counted themselves lucky that their wrathful king chose only dwarfs as his closest servants and so the little fellows were the ones always within reach when the king felt like venting his royal anger, which was often. The king had the anger of a wild bull in a rodeo bent on throwing off the irritating cowboy straddling his back.

The king was now waiting anxiously for Mobuh. With his left foot, he shoved the writhing dwarf from his side and beeped again for his chief minister.

Mobuh, the chief minister, was a plump old man who always looked as if he was smiling, despite the constant stress of coping with king Awobwa's outbursts of anger. He looked like a bald duck and gulped down his food like a hippopotamus when he was at table. It was alleged that when Mobuh's mother was pregnant with him, it was generally believed that she was going to have triplets or quadruplets, even after the doctors had determined that there was just one foetus. When Mobuh finally came out alone, stories about his birth circulated among the ordinary folk who still believed that Mobuh's mother should have had more than one baby. Rumours went round that on the birth of Mobuh alone, the doctor suspected that with his sheer size and weight of about ten kilograms, he might have suffocated the other babies to death inside the womb. One raconteur even insisted that an attending nurse had suggested that they check inside the womb to find out whether the fellow siblings were not taking cover, preferring to stay there instead of coming out to join the brother who had suffocated them for so long inside the womb. Whatever the case, said the rumour mongers had it that the doctor looked for a scope and checked inside the massive womb in vain for any signs of another baby, dead or alive.

As a grown man, Mobuh had considered his massive size when choosing a wife. Mrs. Mobuh was terribly overweight even as a young bride. After giving birth to two children she had become something close to an elephant in human form. Her voluptuous breasts and ample backside compelled the Mobuh couple to acquire a special bed reinforced with the best steel. Before their children grew up to adulthood, they already looked like juvenile copies of the couple. The heavy appetites they had even as children had always been satiated because their father was a senior statesman who had access to all the food such ravenous eaters could possibly need.

Mobuh waddled in diffidently and stood waiting for King Awobua to say why he was needed. The sight of the bleeding dwarf on the floor by the window comforted him. That was proof that the royal anger had been soothed.

"You wanted to see me, my lord?" he chirped. Mobuh had one of those high pitched voices, possibly due to a throat constricted by too much fat around it.

"Yes!" growled king Awobua. "Take a look at the screen."

Mobuh turned respectfully towards the screen and observed an earthling who, though still unsteady on his legs, was helping another earthling, a female it seemed and quite dazed, to get up.

"What do you make of that?" continued King Awobua;

"Sir?" Mobuh was confused by what he was seeing.

"Do I have to bring out you eyeballs and rub in that damned earth scene before you see it?" barked the king.

"I was simply shocked and surprised sir. I can see everything clearly."

"Good," said the king "and let it sink into your thick skull."

King Awobua's life goal was to conquer the earth. He was king of Mungongoh, a small, rocky satellite that revolved around Mars, just like the moon revolves round the earth. Although Mungongoh was further away from the sun than the earth, there was constant daylight. Apart from the sun, many other stars provided light from safe distances. Mungongoh was not fertile and was becoming overpopulated. It was slightly smaller than the moon but with an almost even surface. There were no seas and rivers in Mungongoh apart from a few crater lakes where very limited and controlled fishing was done. Because of the rocky nature of the soil, very little pasture was available where dwarf cattle grazed alongside other small ruminants that looked like goats and sheep. There were very few birds and this deficiency was compensated for by an abundance of insects. The few farms that existed were just enough to produce the meagre sustenance that the people subsisted on, and it was only possible through very improved farming systems. Everything in Mungongoh belonged to the king, and all was planned such that its citizen had access to the basics that enabled them to live. The system of communism in the Soviet Union could have learnt a lesson or two from their system of state control. However, like in most societies, even in the utopia assumed in scientific communism, there was some class distinction. The privileged class had access to every comfort, and food in abundance.

Their language, Intangikom, was musical and lacked certain letters like 'P' and 'L'. They had very beautiful songs and even the males sang with such angelic voices that they did not need to be castrated in their child hood for the purpose of singing beautifully.

Mungongoh was one big city without any villages, apart from the outskirts, where there were clusters of communities somewhat reminiscent of Earth villages.

6

The people of Mungongoh had a long history. They had occupied the planet of Mars for billions of years, alongside other peoples. There had been abundant land out there, rich and fertile, producing much food and livestock. Everybody lived in luxury and comfort and this led to a rapid and steady increase in population. One of the strongest points of the inhabitants of Mars at that time was their interest in scientific research. Improvement in the scientific sphere had thus been considerable and nuclear weapons had been discovered on Mars when dinosaurs still roamed the earth. This rapid development led to some negative results. Since there were several kingdoms on Mars, rivalries had been rife, with kingdoms jostling against one another for supremacy. This competition for power and domination had eventually led to an explosive and destructive nuclear war. All nations on earth would cease their bellicose posturing and scamper to safety if they had only the briefest of glimpses of the devastation that warmongering by people with more firepower than sense had brought to Mars. The whole planet was laid to waste and became uninhabitable. All life perished. Well, not all life, actually. Mungongoh, which was one of the kingdoms on Mars, was ruled at the time by a very clever king who had had the ingenious idea of developing a fleet of specially constructed spaceships in anticipation of such an explosion. The spaceships looked very much like saucers. Their form of propulsion involved the spinning of these vessels at an unimaginable speed. The vehicles were fully equipped with every item that would make life away from Mars comfortable. They were equally stacked with household items, food items, items of leisure and whatever was considered important. While the other kings spent fortunes on nuclear arms, the king of Mungongoh invested in a solid defence system that would permit smooth take-off from the planet in case of war. Even then, when the apocalypse erupted, the people of

Mungongoh were not quite prepared. They would certainly have loved to move further away to some very comfortable place where life would have been as pleasant, or near as pleasant as could be possibly managed, to life on Mars. The suddenness with which the war had escalated and the sheer force and rapidity of the whole thing had compelled the king to bundle his people into the waiting crafts for a premature take off for the rocky satellite of Mars which happened to be closest. They finally landed on the desolate satellite, where it had been assumed that their stay would be short lived. They had had no major crises or accidents along the way apart from the loss of two space ships. The satellite was inhabited only by some primitive dwarfs who were easily subdued.

The dwarfs were the original occupants of Mungongoh. They were stunted fellows without any hair. They therefore neither had eye brows and lashes nor beards. Their large bald heads were crowned with a very flat top, very appropriate for their use as side stools for the king. Their stunted bodies had two short arms and two short legs, but without thighs. The dwarfs were pure red in colour and quite sturdy. Dwarfs had roamed the lands of Mungongoh freely for eons until the sudden arrival of the Martian folk. For some unknown reason, there were about ten male dwarfs to one female. They thus practiced a primitive form of polyandry. This was possibly the reason for their small population. They had a very rudimentary form of civilization, only slightly better than what obtained among the Neanderthals.

When the far more advanced and numerous Mungongoh people arrived, they easily subdued the dwarfs, captured many of them for use as slaves. Given the very limited numbers the captured dwarfs, they were reserved to serve only the kings, and this continued right to the era of King Awobua.

8

Although there had been no real struggle in the process of capturing the dwarfs, quite a number of them had escaped under a female leader called Fuam and now lived underground, just like moles. The people of Mungongoh did not think that they posed any threat so they left them alone.

Dwarfs were not subject to natural death and would continue living if not confronted by extreme violence. This tied in with their slow reproduction rate, as some dwarfs born thousands of years ago still lived. Dwarfs in Mungongoh mainly died when struck violently by relatively larger Mungongoh citizens, or when eaten by lions. Since the dwarfs in the wild were considerably safer in their underground hideouts, their numbers increased considerably over time, enabling them to muster a serious guerrilla group in their underground abode. Fuam had become a great general and the dwarfs were only waiting for the right opportunity to strike.

They would never forget the time when they owned Mungongoh and roamed undisturbed, going freely wherever they wanted. They were equally aware of the plight of their kind who had been captured and used as slaves by the Mungongoh kings. The previous kings had been better, but the current one was a monster and his regular escapades with dwarfs were reported to them on daily basis. Fuam had built a formidable underground force and their vengeance, when it came, would be terrible.

Since the people of Mungongoh had no impression that trouble could be brewing somewhere in the bowels of Mungongoh, life continued as usual, with the king wasting away as many dwarfs as his unlimited anger warranted.

Everybody in Mungongoh was aware of the harsh treatment the dwarfs received each time the king went off his rocker. Like Cleopatra's food tasters, dwarfs stood the risk of losing their lives at any moment. Their privileged role of cushioning the king's anger exposed them to so much viciousness given the very regular angry tantrums of King Awobua. He fed them very well, no doubt, but pounced on them mercilessly at each outburst of anger. The sages of the land had advised the king that he could groom dwarfs for this purpose instead of hammering dangerously on the skulls of his own citizens.

After a while, a further assessment of the situation convinced the king that another migration might prove disastrous, so he decided to stay on. The satellite, which the dwarfs had dubbed Jvatein, was rechristened Mungongoh as a link between the old nation in Mars and the new abode.

Mungongoh was not the ideal place for settlement but conditions there were certainly better than what currently prevailed on Mars. A reverse situation now obtained, with a habitable satellite and an inhabitable planet, just like what might happen to the inhabitants of the earth if suddenly a global nuclear war compelled them to transfer to the moon, where conditions would be better than conditions on a barren earth full of radioactive substances. But then, despite the situation of brinkmanship on earth, the earthlings were still reined in by cowardice and had never gone overboard in their squabbling over who would dominate the world. On the other hand it was possible that the slower pace of scientific development on earth had saved it from global catastrophe, and permitted some degree of peace and understanding to prevail despite the arms race. Conditions on earth were therefore still better than on Mungongoh.

This was tempting King Awobua to covet the earth the way the president of a former French colony would covet the position of the president of France. His dream was to eliminate the earth's population without destroying any property and to transfer the people of Mungongo to the earth. King Awobua was fully aware of the great difficulty of this task of taking over the earth and was prepared to spend as much wealth and effort as possible to achieve this aim. So he had created the Institute for Research and Development of Ideas for the taking over of the Earth, simply known as the IRDI. This institution had a membership of fifty, and twenty of them were females. It was involved in research and the development of ideas that could enable the king to destroy the earth's population. It had the best scientists and professors as members and resembled something like the Politbureau of the Central Committee in the Soviet Union's communist party. This was a highly privileged group of persons. They had access to every benefit and comfort in Mungongoh. Since the members of this distinguished institution were specialists in various fields, many of them employed agents and spies, and these were well trained for information-gathering and forms of infiltration on earth to foster the aims of the members of the IRDI. These ferrets were often sent down to earth, where they roamed around collecting every little bit of useful information.

Armed with thorough knowledge of the earth and a rich store of ideas collected from other planets, they had analyzed a great deal of data and developed ideas to enable the king to destroy the earth's inhabitants and take over. Although a few of the initial ideas succeeded in causing much harm on earth, many were of little consequence.

At one point, for example, Mungongoh succeeded in pushing the people of the earth to such a point of decadence that their God had been compelled to punish them with the deluge. The people of Munongoh had thought that their chance had come, but a simple man called Noah, who had foreseen everything, constructed a large ark with which mankind was saved. Wars were provoked but only on two occasions did they even reach a global scale. Destructive drugs like heroin and cocaine were introduced, but they did not succeed in spreading dangerously to all the corners of

11

the world. The scientists of Mungongoh had even attempted to use natural phenomena like eruptions, landslides, and bush fires, but none of these attempts ever reached the required scale.

After several failed attempts, a tall female academician with a striking resemblance to a praying mantis had proposed the use of locusts to destroy all food and starve the earthlings to death. Her argument was simple. Locusts were very migratory and could spread quickly all over the world. Locusts were ravenous feeders and did not spare any greenery. If locusts landed in the fields, orchards and gardens of the earthlings, they would eat up every existing leaf. The idea was hotly defended by two males who consumed locusts on a regular basis.

After a vote, the locust idea had been adopted and presented to King Awobua. He had been convinced by Mobuh about the practicality of the idea and the certainty of its success. The king himself had thought it was an idea worth trying and had ordered Mobuh to make available ample funds for the program. A special breeding project for locusts had been set up and tons of locusts were produced and sent down to the earth. The first lot fell around the area now covered by Mauritania, Mali, Niger and Chad and King Awobua was happy to see the area transformed from lush farms of sorghum and maize into an expanse of sand. The Sahel and parts of the Sahara were thus created and expanded as more locusts were dispatched to parts of the area now covered by Libya, Morocco, Tunisia, Algeria and Egypt. Some swarms settled further south on the continent of Africa, specifically in the area now known as Namibia, and after eating up everything, left behind an arid wasteland. The swarms then migrated across the Pacific Ocean to the land of the Aborigines and transformed vast expanses of fertile land into the Great Australian Desert. America was not spared as the locusts cleared off all vegetation around part of the present California, creating a desert that stretched into what is now known as Mexico. Some swarms even dared the great Amazon forest but could only succeed in creating the small Atacama Desert. Since the locust dispatch was not well coordinated, many areas completely escaped the locust invasion, while some had repeated locust invasions. The area around Arabia, Kazakhstan, Turkistan, Kyrgyzstan and Afghanistan received double doses of the locust attack.

Although insecticides had not been developed by then, the strategy was bound to fail. Certain basic aspects had been overlooked in its formulation. The disorganized dispatch of locusts had ended up in repeated attacks in some areas and this resulted in the careless death of huge swarms from hunger as they landed on areas where every form of sustenance for them had been cleared off. Many swarms headed for the North Pole, Greenland, Siberia and Alaska and simply perished from the very harsh conditions. Those that landed in equatorial Africa and the Amazon area had a serious challenge with the dense equatorial forests and ended up as prey for birds, animals and reptiles. One year after the locust program was unleashed, its shortcomings became apparent and reluctantly, the king had to call it off.

The cranky academician who had developed it was thrown to the lions as a lesson to others that they should not raise the king's hopes only to dash them shortly after.

Another academician and researcher had come up with something else. Although being offered to the lions in case of failure was a clear and present danger, the glory and fame that awaited the lucky tough egg who would come up with just the right idea was very much coveted. The researcher had developed a terrible disease which he called syphilis. This disease, which could be easily transmitted, had no cure. It was transmitted through sex and the constant wars that raged around the world always went hand-in-hand with a lot of sex and rape as lustful soldiers attacked the women of the vanquished. It would spread widely from soldiers, to prostitutes and housemaids, and further to frivolous wives and husbands. Sailors would take it from Europe to Africa, Asia and across the Pacific, while traders would take it by caravan to Arabia and parts of Asia. Like other bright ideas before it, this one met with failure. Syphilis did not spread fast enough and a cure was discovered sooner than the initiator of the strategy had expected.

Some of the destructive ideas were repeated with greater success, but always developed a serious flaw along the line. After the bubonic plague or the Black Death had ravaged parts of the world and a cure was eventually discovered, the great Fire plague was developed and unleashed upon the world. The name 'fire plague' was derived from the burning sensation that tortured the afflicted person until death. Unlike the bubonic Fire plague that had been transmitted from infected animals or persons by fleas, this Fire plague could be transmitted simply by eating food that a contaminated rodent had sniffed or nibbled. Since rats never went past any edible thing in their path without sniffing at it, the rate of transmission was quite high. This had received great applause from King Awobua who had been assured by Mobuh that it was most certainly a winner. The system of transmission of this deadly pestilence was easy. Rats would be infected and sent down to the earth. Cockroaches had been considered, but the constant use of insecticides by some heartless earthlings reduced the chances of cockroaches ever getting into their homes. Domestic animals too had been considered, but information from spies on earth stated that domestic animals could only go where the earthlings took or allowed them, thus considerably limiting their capacity to spread the disease.

A few rats had been infected with the Fire plague and sent through special courier to the earth. The dispatch system was easy. Rats were put in special containers and made to hibernate just like bears in winter. Then, they were transported in small un-manned space crafts that were not meant to return to Mungongoh and were designed to self-destruct immediately after delivering their cargo of deadly rats to the earth. On earth they were reanimated and deposited where they would easily mingle with earth rats. Rats moved all over the earth and would in no time spread the disease to all the corners of the earth. Rats from Europe got to Africa, Asia and America through ships, hobnobbed with local rats and mice of these areas, and stood every chance of spreading the Fire plague.

The results had been devastating. The Fire plague had spread like wildfire and was wiping out the earth's population at an alarming rate. King Awobua had been certain that in less than a year, the earth would be totally his. He had even promised his officials of the Institute of Research and Development of Ideas (to take over the earth) – IRDI – the highest award in the land, which was the Order of *Wulu Tuh*. Awobua's consternation was therefore clearly understandable when he saw earthlings apparently recovering instead of dying.

"Can you explain this to me?" he barked at Mobuh

"It cannot be, Sir. I am sure they will soon collapse and die."

"Collapse and die?" King Awobua snorted. "Can't you see that they are actually getting up?"

King Awobua went over to the screen and switched it off.

"I will have all of you flogged for this, as a form of warning," he threatened. "You know quite well what I can do when I get really angry. It would appear that senior officials taste better to my baby lions."

The king sat down, still glowering at Mobuh;

"Or you have some sound explanation to give?" he asked

"I suppose we should summon Ngess, Sir" said the quivering Mobuh.

Ngess was a lame man who limped very badly and was thus generally classified among the downtrodden. This made everybody overlook his other qualities until they were in dire straights. He was actually a very intelligent man with a high IQ, a man who had the ability to assess situations correctly and predict the right outcome. But, like Cassandra in ancient Troy whose predictions were never believed until after they had come to pass, his opinion was always sought only after a presumed impeccable idea had failed. It had never occurred to the head of IRDI to make him a member of the institution. After all, he was not a professor and could never be expected to be capable of proposing anything worth considering.

King Awobua considered the idea and seemed to agree with it.

"Send for him then," commanded the king.

2

Mobuh removed a small communication device from his breast pocket and buzzed Ngess, who answered promptly. The device looked like our cell pones on earth but you did not need to go to the trouble of keying in numbers before getting to who ever you were calling. You simply thought about the person and the link connected. Of course, the capacity and range of the phone depended on whom it was designed for. Ordinary persons like Ngess could only communicate within Mungongoh. Members of IRDI and other very senior officials like Mobuh carried devices that could call across the Milky Way. These gadgets were personal and could not be offered as a gift. However, special ones were designed for agents who were sent out on mission to the earth. With these phones, they could easily communicate with those officials in Mungongoh whose phones could call across the Milky Way.

When Ngess heard that the king himself wanted to see him, he dropped everything he was doing and limped to the palace. It was very rare for the king to see or talk to any one apart from Mobuh. The palace guards knew Ngess very well and were aware that he was always summoned when something had gone wrong. He was thus allowed to rush in unperturbed. He was ushered into the inner sanctum of king Awobua by a stern-looking attendant who looked as if he would not let such riff raff into the presence of the king if it were left to him. On beholding the king, Ngess bowed respectfully and waited for him to talk. It was Mobuh, however, who broached the topic.

"Ngess do you know why I have summoned you?"

"Not until you tell me sir" Ngess answered meekly.

"Were you aware of our latest strategy to wipe out those idiots from the surface of the earth?"

"Using the Fire plague, Sir? Yes, I heard about it, an ingenious idea sir, but as porous as a tea sieve".

"You knew this strategy would not work?" roared king Awobua.

"Yes sir." Ngess was trembling like a tree leaf in a high wind. However, he summoned up some courage and continued.

"From my analysis I realised that the strategy will not work, but no one would listen to me".

"Let's hear your reason for the failure of the strategy, then."

Encouraged, Ngess cleared his throat and commenced.

"The idea indeed was ingenious. Rats have the ability to enter any vehicle: ship, aircraft, you name it. They can easily penetrate into any home, office, church, etc. so long as grain, tubers, and any other material that serves as food to rats is present. There are also many rats in the wild that roam distances foraging for food. Yes, the idea of spreading a deadly disease through rats was ingenious."

"I did not call you to come and defend a failed strategy," grumbled the king. "If you continue babbling about ingenious strategies, I will treat you like one of my dwarfs." The king glowered.

Ngess immediately adjusted, and continued.

"The problems with the strategy are many."

"Go straight to the point," bellowed King Awobua impatiently. "I watched Fire plague-stricken fellows resurrecting. How do you explain that?"

"The main problem with the strategy was the timing. You can't expect rats to go everywhere in winter. The winter temperature is quite cold. It renders many parasites and viruses inactive. In this particular case, the Fire plague virus was weakened by the freezing weather and could not perform as it was expected to."

Ngess paused to see how his point was taken.

"You mean we would be successful if this attack takes place in summer?" the king asked.

"Not fully. Summer in Europe and North America means winter in the Southern part of the globe. Besides, the people of the earth have been working on vaccines and other preventive measures. By summertime they would be quite prepared if another bout of Fire plague were unleashed upon them. You realise sir, the earthlings already succeeded in getting a cure for the bubonic plague that was equally as deadly"

King Awobua looked at him speculatively. The blighter was actually dismissing a grandiose plan with a few words. It had cost several billion *kuo* to put up the rat and Fire plague project and its failure was most galling. *Kuo* was the currency in Mungongoh and unlike our money on earth which is printed on paper, it was produced on expensive cloth. *Kuo* had sub units just like cent in the dollar, the shilling in the pound and the kopek in the rouble. *Kuo* had *kaba* and *deli*. The *kaba* and the *deli* were minted on special marble.

"Why don't you propose a better option, a sound strategy that cannot fail?" suggested the disappointed king.

It was then that Mobuh, who had been quiet all this while stepped in.

"It won't do, your majesty. Ngess never has any idea or strategies to offer. He simply steps in like one of those academic critics who are not capable of writing a simple story, but criticize masterpieces that took years to work out. Ngess's talents only surface when well thought-out strategies have failed."

Awobua did not bother to ask when Ngess had ever been consulted before the developing of any strategy. Ngess, for his part, would never have had the courage to point this out, so he remained humbly silent.

"In that case, you'd better take off. Get out of the palace before I get my guards to offer you to my lion pets."

The lion pets, as he fondly called, them were ferocious animals that always seemed hungry despite the amount of care they received in terms of nourishment. Many disfigured dwarfs, and citizens of Mungongoh who were suspected of treason ended up inside them.

Way back in Mars, where there had been some abundance, these lions had served like white elephants in Siam. They were a sign of status, class and royalty. All the monarchs herd large collections of them and gave them to worthy nobles as a sign of appreciation. The lions were well fed and admired but served no other purpose.

When the clever king of Mungongoh in Mars was preparing for the catastrophe that had come to pass, he had not forgotten the lions. One of the flying saucers prepared for emergency take-off was designed to hold as many lions as possible. After the community had landed and settled in Mungongoh, the lions had been kept in special cages. Eventually, feeding them became a problem and it was finally resolved that their numbers be reduced to a hundred and all of them rendered sterile, apart from one female and male that were kept for procreation.

When Awobua came to the throne, however, he gave the lions his special love and protection. The beasts had tripled in number and there was no longer any restriction on their reproduction processes.

This had caused a lot of bitterness among the citizens of Mungongoh, whose food rations had dropped due to the ravenous appetites of the lions. Besides, to please these special pets, the king easily condemned Mungongoh citizens to be eaten by them for minor transgressions.

Their other use as a form of entertainment introduced by the king was rather repulsive to a people who, unlike humans, did not quite enjoy watching individuals punching each other savagely in a boxing ring, or gladiators fighting to death or being mauled by ferocious beasts in a Roman circus.

After dismissing Ngess, King Awobua turned to Mobuh.

"You and your researchers should come up with a better strategy soon. You know how much *kuo* it costs me to keep all those spies on earth."

"We will do our best, Sir," promised Mobuh.

"At times, I wonder whether you will not make a good meal for my lions. That exaggerated waistline, ample backside and potbelly of yours would make a choice meal for them, a special treat, you know."

"I am a very loyal citizen sir, Mobuh said.

"I know that very well," replied the king "If you weren't, my lions would have feasted on you a long time ago."

The king smacked his lips and picked up a large cricket from the tray of snacks in front of him.

"But remember that there is a limit to everything. You know that you can suddenly cease to become my favourite assistant if I so decide."

"I know that, Sir," replied the shaken Mobuh. "I have always declared my unshakable allegiance to you and will always do. I am indeed sorry that we failed you again."

"Again?" roared the king. "This is the umpteenth time you are failing me and you simply say, 'again'?"

"My apologies, Sir," stammered Mobuh. "I am a bit confused, Sir."

"I should not work with confused persons," said the king. "What you are saying is that I should have you replaced."

"No, Sir!" Mobuh rushed to respond. "I mean, I am sorry Sir, I should not have replied so hastily."

"Next time, think before you reply hastily," said the king, "or you will make me very angry."

do now, so that could wait. Just then, the phone rang. It was his wife, trying to find out whether he would have stewed cockroaches or flies for dinner. In Mungongoh, every insect or animal was edible and was served as a meal or a snack. The tiny satellite was so small and so rocky that there was little space for keeping many ruminants, birds, or other animals for meat. There was very little fish and other water-borne food as only three small crater lakes existed on the satellite. Anything that looked edible was therefore consumed. Cockroaches, flies, ants, gnats, and all the revolting insects on earth were delicacies to the people of Mungongo.

Mobuh settled for steamed moths and dismissed his spouse to concentrate on important state affairs. He immediately turned on the small screen by his desk and hastily scrolled through scenes of the earth.

Itoff, the head Professor of IRDI took quite some time coming.

Itoff had been the head of IRDI since it was created by King Awobua. He was the brother of Mobuh's wife and thus Mobuh's favourite for the position when it was created. Mobuh had thus easily used his influence with the king and the fact that the king relied on him to present the appropriate candidate. Itoff's gratitude to Mobuh was therefore like that of a faithful dog. Besides, Mobuh had always protected him in front of the king.Itoff was tall and thin and looked quite the opposite of his sister, who had captured Mobuh's heart. He was a doctor of history and had a firm grasp and knowledge of the history of Mungongoh. Before his appointment as the head of IRDI, Mobuh had used his influence to make him the rector of the University of Mungongoh. Mungongoh had only one university where all the important faculties could be found. As rector, Itoff had spotted young Doctor Funkuin, a very pretty and intelligent female who would have made a good wife to him but for the fact that he was already married. His wife was a short, plump female he had met as a young lecturer in the same university.

As head of the IRDI, Itoff was in close contact and collaboration with his boss, Mobuh and expected to be summoned by him at any moment; he was aware of the fact that Mobuh often took umbrage when his summons was not promptly obeyed. He had been lying in bed with his wife, about to have siesta, when the summons came from Mobuh. His attempt to get up was thwarted by his wife, who had other ideas and insisted on having priority over her husband. Itoff's protests about the boss coming first fell on deaf ears.

"Who would disturb that flabby elephant when his wife needs his attention?" Itoff's wife asked "Relax and have fun I am all yours. Have me."

Itoff had finally succumbed to her caressing fingers, her searching lips, and her tongue. He was sure he would have a rough time with Mobuh, but then, a man needs such times from his wife.

As professor Itoff opened the door to Mobuh's office and went in, he was welcomed with a stern glare.

"You took your time!"

"I was in my bath," Itoff lied.

"A bath at this hour?" asked Mobuh sceptically. "And despite my request to see you urgently, you insisted on completing your bath?" Mobuh continued angrily.

"I did everything I could to get here immediately."

Mobuh calmed down a bit. You could not be too hard on an in-law.

"Do you know that the Fire plague strategy which took so many months to develop and costs so much *kuo* has failed?"

"But our monitors show that earthlings are still dying, Sir. Even our spies are still sending in reports of deaths on a large scale."

"Some may be dying, but others are resurrecting."

"I don't understand, Sir"

Mobuh placed a huge finger on a green button in the side of his desk. A wide screen came up on the far off wall and images appeared. He used another button to search, moving from scene to scene of devastation. Itoff watched with satisfaction, wondering why Mobuh was talking of failed strategies.

Suddenly a scene appeared and Mobuh stopped there.

"Watch" he announced importantly.

There, several blokes dressed in white, all wearing masks and plastic gloves, with microscopes, test tubes and an array of complicated lab equipment in front of them, were working on something that looked serious.

'These," explained Mobuh, "are human scientists. They are well protected against our Fire plague and are working towards vaccines that will save human kind."

Itoff was shocked.

"We never thought of that," he admitted.

Mobuh continued with his search. Several scenes came up where rats were being eliminated by masked men using fire. Finally, they came to a hospital scene. Desperate patients were being attended to by harried doctors and nurses, all wearing masks and gloves. Some beds had the inert bodies of patients who had just died. Others were occupied by patients in their death throws. The devastation was great.

"I am still looking for what I really want you to see," Mobuh said, searching.

He suddenly brightened up as a couple came up on the screen. The man was struggling dazedly to lift the woman onto a bed. From every appearance, they were farmers, and struggling inside their hut.

"These people have the Fire plague, and had almost gotten to the point of no return. Somehow the virus that hit them had been slightly weakened and will instead serve

26

like a vaccine. From every indication, they will not die of the Fire plague. They will recover and will develop immunity against the Fire plague. Their case is not unique."

Itoff sat down, confused. It was quite clear that the Fire plague strategy had failed.

He and his colleagues had doffed their hats to one another in respect when the Fire plague had been dispatched to the earth through a few infected rats. The first pictures from the earth had been very appropriate. The death toll had been very heavy and the Fire plague was spreading to the ends of the earth. In this bliss, the members of the Institute had never thought of possible failure.

"You now realize that King Awobua has every right to be angry, don't you?" Mobuh said.

"The king is already aware of this?" Itoff whispered, quite frightened.

"Yes of course, and he has destroyed one dwarf to cool his anger before meeting you bumbling scientists. You see what a gracious and considerate king you have? He has cooled his anger a bit with the dwarf."

"Nobody has ever doubted the kindness and understanding nature of our king, Sir" Itoff hurried to concur.

"Now, go back and summon all those lazy scientists of yours. I want you to come up with another idea, an ingenious one this time that will not fail, so that we can present it to the king. I give you one week."

Itoff rushed back to his office immediately and started making arrangements for the next meeting of tough eggs. He also planned to be part of any new idea to guarantee its solidity. He was seriously considering an idea one promising young scientist had developed and proposed to him through Dr. Funkuin. The idea concerned the use of a bomb that, if exploded on earth, would clear off all the earthlings and leave everything else upright. Dr. Funkuin, who was an expert in hate sciences, had explained how the bomb would

"That is precisely why I asked for the two of you" said professor Itoff. We are going to go through your idea, eliminate any possible shortcomings, and present it to the IRDI for approval. I am sure King Awobua will be quite satisfied."

They went into a thorough assessment of the idea, after the young man had presented it in vivid detail. Professor Itoff asked several questions and received deft responses from the young man. Funkuin too seemed to understand the whole idea well and contributed where necessary. She was really excited. Finally, Itoff concluded that it was a very solid idea and would not fail like the preceding ones. He would comfortably attach his name to this one as one of the initiators. Pushing it through IRDI was not going to be difficult. Lesser ideas had sailed through. He was already imagining Mobuh and the king smiling gracefully and congratulating him effusively for a job well done.

4

The next meeting of the IRDI was attended by intelligent-looking scholars, most of them with determined looks on their faces. Some had scanty grey hair; others had dyed hair, while others were completely bald. The main aspect common to most of the men was that they could not be considered handsome. They were all dressed in colourful *dallas* and caps of similar material. Two of the females among them looked like witches out of a fairy tale. Itoff, who sat presiding at the head of the table, had the appearance of a chief wizard presiding over a feast where they served human flesh as the plat de jour and offered blood in place of choice wine.

"For our meeting to take off", announced professor Itoff to the assembled group of intellectuals, "Dr Keawi will lead us in praises to our great king."

The people of Mungongoh were very practical and would not believe in a god that was not palpable. Since people are always inclined to worship something, they settled on their king. It was thus a normal thing to call on the king when you got up from bed, to ensure you had a nice day. You called on him before meetings and gatherings and even children sang praises to him before classes.

"Let us praise," said Dr Keawi, standing up.

Everybody followed suit as Dr. Keawi cleared his throat.

"Oh gracious King Awobua! We thank you for agreeing to be the king of this planet. You are the best leader we could ever have, and may you achieve our greatest aim of taking over the earth from those worthless humans. We will always revere you and abide by all your wishes and command. Thank you for the inspiration you have given us that will enable us surface with the most impeccable idea that will enable you clear off the surface of the earth for us to take over and inhabit."

As usual, there was thundering applause, and none of the tough eggs ever bothered to remember that the same prayer was offered every time a new impeccable idea was about to be developed, and the idea always ended up with a flaw.

Professor Itoff took over the floor and held forth.

"As usual, we are very democratic with our procedures. One of us tables the smart idea that he or she has developed and all of us see whether it is sound enough to be adopted or not. Remember that the previous idea had looked perfect and unbeatable, but ended up with flaws which we overlooked. We have failed our good king. This new idea should therefore be considered seriously. It should also be noted that I am part of this new idea and will personally present part of it."

Since Itoff himself claimed that he had participated in the development of this new idea, the general tendency was to consider it as wonderful and everybody listened closely as Itoff continued

"For my part, I think this new idea is watertight. You are expected to see the ingenuity of the idea and give it the support it deserves."

He looked round to see if any scientist dared challenge him and continued.

"This powerfully developed idea has dismissed animals as a possible route through which we could spread death to all the corners of the earth. Animals have proven to be unreliable when it comes to spreading death all over the world. We have thus opted for an explosive idea that does not have the limitations that animals often face in certain circumstances. But remember, we don't want anything destroyed. We have thus come up with another option which is sure to give satisfaction."

"I hope this new idea will not be leaked to the humans, thus enabling them to prepare a timely countermeasure. I don't completely trust some of our agents on earth. They already seem to be enjoying the way of the humans".

This contribution came from an old egghead with a nose like a hornbill. He looked more like one of those dubious and calculating grand viziers who are always scheming to overthrow the caliph.

"We have full confidence in our spies," Professor Itoff rebuked him. "A spy has to fit in completely. Even among the earthlings it is the same. If an American spy has to operate among the pygmies, they choose a dwarf, paint him black and teach him the pygmy language. British language teachers earn huge salaries training Russian spies to speak like the English. A spy even ends up enjoying the delicacies of the people in the area where he operates, even if it is baby shit or dog vomit. No more careless talk about our spies," Itoff warned sternly.

He turned to Dr Funkuin, who was waiting expectantly to be called upon to talk.

"Doctor Funkuin," said Itoff loudly, "read out the new idea which we developed after so much brainstorming."

Dr. Funkuin turned and looked at Itoff with a hint of adoration. It was commonly suspected within the circle of academicians that a secret affair was going on between them.

"Yes, Professor" she said, making every effort to cover any indication of affection.

"After reviewing the limitations of rats as a means of spreading the deadly Fire plague all over the world, we came to the conclusion that our next strategy should be one that should not rely on any thing for which an antidote or countermeasure could be developed. Rat poisons and vaccines are being rapidly developed to check the spread of the Fire plague and the movement of rats, and that is why rat invasions and the Fire plague could not spread far and fast enough. What we need is something that is unstoppable and of lightning efficiency."

Funkuin removed her horned rimmed spectacles, wiped them carefully, and replaced them on her face.

"All of you sitting here are aware of the fact that our king's greatest wish is to wipe out the human race from the surface of the earth. The core of Hate Sciences revolves around how unfairly Mungogoh citizens have been treated since they left Mars, while on the other hand, their closest neighbours on earth have far much more than they need and deserve. When our ancestors landed here from Mars, they considered this place a temporary stopover. Despite our extremely long stay here, the idea of continuing to a more conducive place has not been abandoned. Our king has discovered in the earth that place. The earth is not too far off and easily reachable. Our many missions to the earth have proven beyond doubt that we can conveniently live there. It is time we too had our own chance on earth before those greedy earthlings destroy it. They undeservedly have so much food, while we are virtually starving here. Do you imagine that in some parts of the earth they don't eat chameleons, toads and agama lizards because they have an abundance of beef and mutton? It is scandalous to think that while we are starving on Mungongoh, they bury dead horses, dogs and cats on earth. What a waste!"

There was a general murmur of apprehension.

Inspired, Dr Funkuin continued.

"With all this abundance and easy life, humans are still very stingy and selfish. They still want to conquer each other and have everything. One group is talking about communism where they claim there will be an almost equal distribution of wealth, yet they have ended up with a privileged class.

The others prefer a dog-eat-dog situation where the winner takes it all. Do you imagine that five of the richest men on earth control more wealth than 50 of the poorest countries on the same earth? Anyway, the situation works in our favour. The humans, in their greed, started a cold war amongst themselves. They are virtually at each other's throats."

"I hope you are leading to some thing important" interrupted a shifty-eyed academician who always snoozed off during long meetings.

"You'd better keep quiet and listen," snapped Dr Funkuin, and continued.

"Because of their bellicose nature and total mistrust of each other, the humans are spending huge amounts of their resources on destructive arms. They are now at the level of weapons of mass destruction and have even come up with the atomic and hydrogen bombs. These are weapons that could serve us very well in the elimination of the human race, but the destruction would be so great that there would be nothing useful on earth for us to take over."

Funkuin looked round to see if her oratory was having the desired effect. "You all remember from the history of the origin of Mungongoh how greed led some of our forefathers to blow up their prosperous planet, Mars. Today, Mars is nothing but a desolate wasteland, not worth inhabiting by anybody. The earth may soon get to that stage if we don't rush things and clear off those warmongers from it, and we can best do this through the neutron bomb."

Funkuin at this point tapped a youngish chap in a white coat who was sitting by her side on the arm.

"Dr Munteh here will tell you what we intend to do." Having thus concluded, she returned to her seat

Dr Munteh stood up and arranged a sheaf of papers in front of him. He looked like one of those young promising geniuses who would make the inventor of the Atomic bomb,

month, when the effect of the bomb would have dissipated, we can then take over and introduce other animals. The strategy of how the earthlings would be guided into producing the bomb and fighting a devastating third world war with it has been developed by the Doctor of Hate Sciences, and she is very good at it. Everything will work just fine, sir."

"Alright, you people can leave. You have a blank cheque. Put your plan into action and spare no costs in its achievement. Itoff, I am counting on you not to fail me this time".

Mobuh heaved a sigh of relief as they departed. He was already thinking about his wife and his plate of steamed moths. Just then, there was a buzz from King Awobua, so Mobuh dropped everything and hurried to the king.

"Sir?" he said, as an indication that he was already in the king's presence.

King Awobua pointed at the huge screen in front of him.

"Look at those earthlings we were supposed to have wiped out with the Fire plague. They are carrying out cartons of vaccines from that laboratory. When they developed these is difficult to say, but it shows their great ability to cope."

"That is true, Sir" agreed Mobuh humbly. "The dashed humans have learnt how to cope with harsh deserts, severe winters and even pestilences. They have had plagues before and survived."

"Then why did you rascals come up with another plague if you knew that they had some experience in handling them? I would break that mighty skull of yours if I did not restrain myself!" thundered the king.

"The earlier plagues like the bubonic plague, were limited to certain areas sir, and world-wide travelling was not common. Today, we are virtually dealing with a global village, and we counted on that. Besides, the Fire plague spreads faster and is more devastating." Mobuh would go any length to give satisfaction to the king. His position was very much envied by the members of IRDI, who were considered closest to him in rank. Everybody thus seemed to be bent on satisfying the whims of the king without giving any thought to possible consequences. After all, they had no feelings for earthlings, whom they simply considered lucky and greedy.

5

Nyamfuka was waiting outside the palace, in the department of hate affairs. He was not qualified to gain access to the palace and to enter Mobuh's great presence, so he had to wait humbly for Funkuin at her place of work. Funkuin was one of the heads of department in the Ministry of Hatred and Human Antipathy. Nyamfuka was reflecting on his mission. Some missions on earth were risky, but this one was quite easy. It involved getting a beautiful woman to fall for him, a thing he enjoyed very much. Female earthlings were generally quite hot and satisfied males better than Mungohgoh females. Although Funkuin performed almost as well as the humans, she was hardly ever available, so he welcomed every opportunity on earth which involved hanky panky with women.

"You are quite early," Funkuin said when she went back to her office and met Nyamfuka anxiously waiting. "Your extraordinarily prompt reaction to my summons is suspicious."

"But you have always wanted prompt responses to any summons of yours."

"You want to tell me that it is not the chance to wag that tail of yours on earth that has made you so duty-conscious?"

Funkuin licked her lips longingly, but realized there was no time to take advantage of the presence of the young Casanova.

"Make sure that down on earth, you do only what we require of you," she warned. "How far have you gone with that woman?"

"Quite far, Madame."

"Quite far means what? Are you saying that with your he-goat tendencies, you have already had sex with her?"

"Kind of Madame. That was in the line of duty, not for pleasure."

In response to a frown from Funkuin, he continued.

"I was only tying to kiss her, then things happened and I discovered we had gone further than I planned. Since my orders were to achieve something concrete that would get her completely into my power, I simply took the action to that end."

"That is not what we had planned," shouted Funkuin, in the throes of jealousy. "What we planned was for you to get close to this female so that you could use her to sneak the neutron bomb formula into her boss's office, but you went off and enjoyed yourself instead!"

The dangerous turn that the conversation was taking might end up with him losing the juicy assignment, so it was crucial to butter up Funkuin and straighten things up. Nyamfuka decided to take a small risk.

"We could lock the door of the office, and maybe use the toilet?" he looked temptingly at Funkuin "You know you are the best and I always miss you."

"You tempting young buck, I would have you castrated but for the fact that tomorrow you might still come in handy."

The tone of her voice made Nyamfuka more comfortable. She was almost cooing.

"I will work like a knight of old on one of those holy crusades on earth who, after being engaged in ridding the Holy Land of antichrists and villains during the day, spent the night dreaming of the beautiful lady he had left back at home, far away in Britain."

"What a silly comparison," replied Funkuin. "I have never admired those fellows who abandoned beautiful young maidens just to go slaying dragons and destroying hordes

46

of Arabs in a vain bid to defend Christendom. The type of useless things humans engage in!" Funkuin caressed the young man on the chest and continued:

"Make sure you do only your work and return in one piece. No slaying of Arabs and dragons on earth. You may have that whore again in the process of carrying out the mission, but do it mechanically. You are not supposed to enjoy it because it might deviate you from your target."

"But spies have always enjoyed themselves," protested Nyamfuka. "Even humans. I read about a master spy like myself called James Bond, who was always in bed with one enemy woman or another, but always produced good results."

"You are not human. You are from Mungohgoh" Funkuin pointed out.

"But I am supposed to be operating on earth and with a human woman. I should therefore do like this James Bond."

"You may be right, but don't forget that James Bond always made love to those lasses with one eye open, prepared for any surprises".

"But you can't fully enjoy love making like that," Nyamfuka said.

"May I remind you again, young man that you are not supposed to enjoy it?"

Nyamfuka gave up.

"Okay, give me the formula and the human money; you know they don't use *kuo* on earth."

"What would you want, euros, pounds sterling or dollars?"

"Dollars would be fine since I will be operating in America. You may wish me luck."

"What luck do you want when you seem to be going on a pleasure trip? Remember that while you are out there, your mission involves one woman. Don't stray to any other woman unless you have to," Funkuin said sternly. "Now go to my secretary down the corridor; she has everything prepared for you. Just pick them up and piss off. No lingering."

Nyamfuka went off to see Funkuin's secretary. She was a very pretty young woman who was always making advances to Nyamfuka, without realizing that she was treading on very dangerous ground. Funkuin could easily have had her disfigured if she so much as suspected that Nyamfuka had any feelings for the young woman.

Ignoring her charming smile and the lingering manner in which she served him, Nyamfuka took off for the earth port, from which he would be shuttled down to earth. Apart from spies on mission, no citizen of Mungongoh was allowed access to the earth port. It was full of incoming and exiting agents, all assigned to one mission or another. The flying vehicles were like saucers which moved at lightning speed and were hardly ever seen by humans when they landed on earth. A few Mungongoh pilots had faltered with their vehicles, making it possible for some humans to spot them, but the humans had never succeeded in capturing one.

Nyamfuka took his flight down to earth in a sky-blue flying saucer which landed lightly somewhere near Bermuda and released its passengers. From here Nyamfuka teleported himself to Washington DC. He looked for his usual base where he would change into American clothes, a flat that had been rented by a Mungongoh agent in a high-rise building. Getting there was not a problem because he simply teleported himself.

When he arrived at the flat, he removed a brown suit from a cupboard and dressed nattily. Because the gravitational pull in Mungongoh is different from that on earth, Mungongoh citizens always administered an electric shock on themselves when they came down to earth and this enabled them to adjust immediately and move around like any earthling. Nyamfuka brought out a special cable from the cupboard and attached one end to the tip of his penis. The other end, which was like a plug, he inserted into an electricity socket on the wall by the oak cupboard.

48

The shock from the electricity source coursed through him. Nyamfuka could now walk heavily and clumsily like the earthlings and enjoy everything that humans enjoyed. He sat down in a leather sofa and rested for a short while. He realized that he was quite hungry and went to the refrigerator for a bite. Mungohgoh citizens did not spare good food whenever they had the opportunity. Bacon, veal, beefsteaks, mutton and suchlike were scarce luxuries in Mungongoh. And then there was the adored coffee with all its fragrance and lingering, exquisite taste. After a large snack, Nyamfuka set up his plans and proceeded.

His first action was to call professor Small's secretary Ursula, and make an appointment. The pretty secretary was quite excited on hearing his voice and agreed to meet him immediately after work. She had already agreed to stay late in the office that evening with the eminent professor, but Nyamfuka was hot stuff that she would not miss for anything. He had disappeared without trace after their first sexual encounter but had left and impact. She would give the professor some excuse and fly to Nyamfuka's warm arms.

When it was closing time, Ursula went in to the professor's office and told him she had suddenly developed a head ache and had to go home.

"But you cannot do that" protested the professor "I have already called home to tell my wife that I will be working late"

"I am sorry sir" she replied. "The head ache is quite serious. Let us make it for another day"

"Life is short" pointed out professor Small. "Each day lost is something you will never catch up with. Stay with me and I will soothe the ache."

"I have never hesitated when ever you needed my presence. If I ask to go home early today, you must understand me." Ursula said firmly.

Professor Small had to give up. His wife was pleasantly surprised when he got home early.

In the hotel room where Nyamfuka had booked for the week he expected to stay in Washington, Ursula was snuggling close to him. Nyamfuka was still thinking of the best way to introduce the topic of sneaking bomb formulae into the professor's office.

"Your mind seems to be far off" complained Ursula.

Nyamfuka realised that he had to be more careful. He decided to forget about the bomb formula for the day and concentrate on giving Ursula the best.

The next day, Ursula went to work rather late and when confronted by professor Small, complained about the head ache. That evening, professor Small went home again disappointed. The third day, he still had no access to Ursula after work and went home virtually frustrated. That night Nyamfuka decided that he had prepared Ursula enough and thought it was time to introduce the bomb formula. After some exciting lovemaking, he caressed Ursula gently on the cheeks and said

'Dear, would you do something simple for me?"

"Anything you wish" said the satisfied woman "What is it you want?"

"It is rather difficult for me to say. I wonder whether you would believe me."

"Of course my love, I trust you. Now, what is it?"

"Actually, I am a Russian" said Nyamfuka

"A Russian?" said Ursula in surprise "Are you a spy? God forbid! And I have been feeling very free with you. I should have known."

"I was right" said Nyamfuka, pretending to be sad. I knew you would rush to a hasty conclusion and judge me wrongly."

"I am sorry love. Let me hear it all. But it had better be convincing" said Ursula.

"I am quite sincere and I am sure what I am proposing is for the good of your boss and the world. As I already mentioned, I am a Russian and a close aide to the great Russian professor, Krizhizhanovsky. We have been working on a new nuclear weapon of mass destruction and we reported directly to the Kremlin. Our work was top secret. We finally developed a bomb that can eliminate all life and leave everything else intact. You can imagine this weapon in the hands of those hawks in the Kremlin. I considered this and decided that the bomb formula must be destroyed. But then, I reflected further and decided hat such a great discovery should not be destroyed and concluded that the Americans should have it. I am sorry to say, I eliminated the professor and escaped with the formula. I have had the formula with me all along, but you would agree with that I cannot just walk up and hand over the formula to the Americans. They would not believe me. On the other hand, the Russians would be on my rail. After thinking for a while I concluded that professor Small would be the idle person through whom to send in this formula. Mind you, or meeting was coincidental and not linked to the formula. Between us, it was true love at first sight."

"Are you sure?" asked Ursula "You want to say you really love me?"

"With all my heart" replied Nyamfuka. "In fact, I am already certain that I want to spend the rest of my life with you, that is, if you would have me."

"Ooh, how I do love you" said Ursula, kissing Nyamfuka passionately. Then, she transferred to his ears cooing softly.

After a while Nyamfuka realised that he had to take the issue to the end.

"Dear, we have to hand over the formula to professor Small" he said softly.

"Why?" demanded Ursula. "What makes you think that professor Small is the right person to pass through?"

His speciality is nuclear sciences and it would only be normal if he discovered such a bomb. Besides, in his case, you as is personal secretary could easily sneak it into his office and make him believe that he had discovered it in the first place."

"What if he doesn't take the bait?"

"He would" replied Nyamfuka. Is he not a professor? No professor sees a chance like that and lets it go. Please dear, you are the only one who can help me."

"I will do anything for you dear" said Ursula. Where is the formula?"

"Here" said Nyamfuka, handing over a bright edged paper;

The next morning, Ursula placed the formula among some important papers that she knew the professor would read first thing in the morning

When professor Small came in, he frowned at Ursula and hurried to his office without bothering to respond to her greeting. He was still smart from her having left him in the cold for the past four days. As he settled behind his oaken desk, his eyes immediately fell on a strange paper with strong hue on the borders.

From the monitoring posts in Mungongoh things seemed to be moving as planned. The eminent professor had discovered the neutron bomb formula on his table, mixed with other papers, attracted to it by the strong hue on the borders of the paper. After reading through it thoroughly, he had not even bothered to ask his secretary how the thing had come to be lying on his desk. He shouted even louder than Archimedes, although he actually forbore to say 'Eureka', and rushed to declare his achievements to the university administration.

Mobuh watched with glee as CNN showed the Professor being decorated for a job well-done. He buzzed for Itoff when a scene came showing the Russians complaining about the discovery of a capitalist bomb. He was equally aware that the Russians would secretly be rallying their spies to get the formula to them in a hurry.

"Congratulations," he boomed amicably. "Things seem to be moving in the right direction. I am sure in a short while, things will improve."

"I hope the King himself is watching, sir", Itoff said.

"Watching? That is his favourite pastime. He is watching very closely and enjoying every step towards the destruction of the earth."

As the months passed, the Russian were spending a fortune on spies in a bid to get hold of the neutron bomb formula. Apart from the fact that a few of these spies got apprehended by the Americans, the Russians never got it because the Americans guarded the secret of the neutron bombe like a rare jewel. In desperation, the Russians kept ranting about a capitalist bomb and how America was promoting the arms race. The Americans, for their part, were sceptical of the use of any nuclear weapon of a certain capacity without bringing about global catastrophe and preferred to keep their neutron bomb safely away in the arsenals. While King Awobua was waiting anxiously for the Americans to start a war with their new weapon, the president of America, who happened to be a peace loving man, would not have innocent Russians killed just because their leaders were hawks.

6

Six months passed without anything concrete happening apart from the fact that King Awobua was growing increasingly impatient. The Americans kept showing off their new achievements without attempting to provoke an occasion to use it, as the king had hoped. The Russians continued grumbling about it in their news slot *Govorit Moskva* and their main newspaper *Pravda*, but still remained very careful not to provoke the Americans into using the deadly weapon. In his impatience, the King had already destroyed ten dwarfs. Finally, in a bid to put an end to this carnage, King Awobua summoned Mobuh into his inner chambers.

"This is it", Mobuh thought. He too had been closely monitoring the situation and losing patience. He had already called Itoff and given him a piece of his mind. His next step had been to put Ngess on the alert in case the King reached his limit and needed some explanation. As he moved into the King's chambers in response to the summons, with Ngess following closely behind him, his apprehension grew to extremes. A hypertensive royal adviser would have collapsed on the spot. There was no bloody dwarf in the room. This meant that the king's anger had not been contained and could thus land on him. He stepped back defensively.

"Adjust," said the king, showing Mobuh the smashed monitor in front of him. "Have this replaced immediately."

"Yes Sir," said Mobuh trembling, "Immediately, Sir." He began to back out of the room.

7

During the next assembly of sharp brains, Funkuin was as quiet as a chameleon. She was normally of a fiery disposition. This doctor of hate sciences was quite attractive to many of the male members of IRDI. Funkuin was one of those tough females who had succeeded in making it to the top on her own. It is true that professor Itof had stretched out a hand on which she had sprung to the eminent position of member of IRDI, but before he noticed her, she was already struggling hard on her own. She had always handled her projects with dexterity and success. This failed bomb idea was a very big blow to her and the disgrace she had received from the failed project was quite devastating. However, another nutcase had another impeccable idea to present to the IRDI. Like the others before, it sounded irreproachable.

The new wunderkind was a rotund fellow with a double chin, called Fulumfuchong. Actually, Fulumfuchong's features were bland and he was not the type of man that a young girl would defy conservative parents to elope with. However, compared with the pack of stiffnecks in IRDI, he could be considered not ugly.

Apart from that, he was relatively younger than all of them and smarter. He had come from a top class family and thanks to his class and sharpness, had moved up in rank quite fast. Fulumfuchong was an academician and a doctor in aeronautics and nuclear sciences. He had always come first in his class and had maintained this position right through university, where he defended his doctorate thesis with high distinction. Before becoming a member of IRDI, Fulumfochong had been one of the chief design engineers of the centre for construction and repairs of spacecraft. He had designed many of the flying saucers used by Mungongoh agents on special missions, leaving the construction to the less talented designers.

Fulumfuchong was not married and had a special crush on Yivissi, one of the young female members of IRDI, but her beauty and grace made her unapproachable. Besides, her mother controlled and protected her as jealously as a bull would protect the lone cow left on the farm, so that all prospective suitors kept as far away from her as possible.

Fulumfuchong's longing for Yivissi did not interfere with his work. Rather, he worked hard to impress upon her the fact that he was a man of talent. However, his lust for her made him to consider all other women to be without attraction. He had thus remained single, though a very eminent bachelor who was the focus of the fevered imagination of many a Mungongoh female.

"This one cannot fail," he began. "It is not like some far-fetched ideas that have been imposed on us before."

He stopped and stared at Funkuin meaningfully.

"What just happened was quite foolish and unpardonable. What we really should have done after the Fire plague catastrophe, was to examine the Fire plague program closely and see where it went wrong. Maybe it was the choice of animal to serve as a carrier, or maybe it was the choice of pestilence that was the problem. What we have here now is the best idea. Nobody can beat it."

"Lets here it, then," Funkuin said curtly. "It is not dwelling on an introduction that makes an idea carry fire."

The pompous orator turned angrily to Funkuin. "This is not one of those your lousy ideas. You can push humans to create bombs but you cannot force them to use them."

"Let's hear what you have to say, then, that you consider as better."

"We have adopted the idea of the rat and Fire plague, and simply changed the animal and the pestilence." said Fulumfuchong. He made sure that everybody was attentive before continuing.

"Let us start from the angle of the pestilence. There was nothing that pushed humans into the Fire plague. It just came. On the other hand what we are introducing is something that cannot fail. It is based on the fact that all humans like sex and all crave the act that their God invented for procreation. Virtually every human is promiscuous. The men cheat on their women, the women cheat on their men and even the unmarried cheat on their girl or boy friends, and this is done regularly. To crown it all, we have the sex workers who make love as many times a day as they are paid money. Way backing the ancient civilizations on earth the sexual act has been prominent in rituals, activities of entertainment and cultural activities. Right up to today, sexual expressions are common n dances, dressing, adverts, well just all over. Most inhabitants of the earth are voyeurs and all enjoy pornography. They don't have the kind of morals we have here in Mungongoh. We neither have sex workers nor brothels. We prefer to enjoy sex when it is convenient, without any touch of the voyeur or unbridled priapism in us. Yes, we don't consider pornographic films and books to be of any importance, as opposed to the depraved humans who produce and enjoy tons of the stuff. In fact, all humans seem to live for sex."

"Why don't you go to the point instead of beating about the bush?" a raucous voice sounded from one corner.

"Yeah, stop dawdling," added a deep bass

"But I am leading up to the point," protested Fulumfuchong. "Instead of interrupting rudely, you'd better sit quietly and listen.

"I was saying that we have identified a very dangerous and deadly virus which will be spread on earth through sex. Although we have tried as much as possible to make it kill as fast as the Fire plague, we have only succeeded in guaranteeing that any human who gets it will be dead in one year.

"But that is too long," protested a shrill female voice this time. "The king wants to take over the earth right away."

"We have considered all that. However the efficiency of this idea warrants waiting even ten years to see it through."

"So with this new pestilence – how do you call it?"

"We have not really given it a name. We have left it to the humans to give whatever name suits them."

"So with this new pestilence, when these horny humans enjoy what they cherish most, the stuff is transmitted?"

"Exactly," replied Fulumfuchong with emphasis.

"Have you considered the fact that a few people on earth are not capable of having sex?" The probing continued. "Take the case of eunuchs" Fulumfuchong was not a favourite of Itoff, so he preferred to prolong the probing as much as possible.

"That is a good question," Itoff said. "Let us have a good answer to that."

"We have considered that too. That is why we have included every form of blood contact as a likely route through which the virus can be transmitted. Some of these eunuchs take drugs and share needles quite often. In places like Africa where drug addiction is still not very common, a lot of shaving and risky hairdressing is done commonly with the aid of razorblades and other sharp instruments through which blood contact can occur. We have also added easy transmission from mother to child. Eventually, virtually every child in the world will be born already contaminated."

"But it still leaves out respectable old men," an academic who had been quiet up till now said.

"For that" continued Fulumfuchong, "we shall enable the humans to discover a new drug they will call Viagra. You see, most of these old men or senior citizens become respectable and honest with their old wives just because their ability to make love is gone. This Viagra will give them the possibility of having erections when ever they want. You would need to see them spinning around with girls fit to be their granddaughters, when they have a dose of Viagra. Very soon, they will become the biggest spreaders of the disease."

"What of the old retired wives who have decided to give up sex or whose husbands no longer have sex with them?" asked Itoff

"That's no problem. They will not suspect that at that age their husbands would contract the sexually transmitted disease. They will not even believe that he still has the capacity to have sex. When he falls ill, they will be careless in the way they handle him, without thinking of protecting themselves."

It looked like every possible shortcoming was exhausted. But then a thin, tough woman, who looked like an efficient British governess, uncovered another soft spot.

"I suspect you have never heard of certain religious denominations on earth where the men and women of the cloth are supposed to be celibate, and they are so many. How do you think this killer disease will spread to them, given the fact that they have all taken the vow of chastity?" She asked.

There was a general murmur as this new problem was considered by all the members present, but it was immediately quashed by Fulumfuchong.

"The question of how it will spread to them or among them does not hold at all. In fact the disease will be spread by them."

"How?" the question came in a chorus.

"The vow of chastity is just a vow, a thing that nobody follows. It is just like nurses and doctors taking the Hypocritic Oath".

"Hippocratic Oath, you mean?" chirped a cross eyed professor.

"Yeah, whatever it is. Medics take this oath and the moment they start working in hospitals, they go for the money rather than the respect of the oath".

"But what has that got to do with men and women of the cloth? You should see how pious many of them look. I wonder whether they would go for a baseless thing like sex."

"The God of the earth created sex and designed it to be very enjoyable. For the church to completely deprive individuals of it is not correct. It gives room to a lot of illegal sex, fornication and adultery. These are all crimes that easily lead to abortions and infanticide which are even worse than simple sex. Other Christians have recognized this danger, and allow their men and women of the cloth to marry. That way they can enjoy this wonderful free gift of God, which is sex, the right way. However we are not here to criticize what happens on earth. We are rather concerned with spreading our killer disease."

"What ever you say" said a thick set woman, there are still some priests and nuns that have withdrawn completely from sex as their religion dictates. Not all earthlings are oversexed."

"That is quite true" said Fulumfuchong "and apart from them, we also have lots of very shy earthlings who may never sum up the courage to request for sex from a woman or from a man. We have a solution for this. We have thought of something that will increase the libido of this earthlings to such an extent that shyness or respect for abstention from sex will be cast away by all. We first developed a gas for this purpose, but discovered that the atmosphere of the earth was too vast for it. We have thus developed a liquid that will be introduced into water sources. Just a drop will be enough to transform a thousand pious nuns into raving sexual maniacs."

A bright idea like this and no applause from these dumb fools, thought Fulumfuchong as he turned over to the next page.

"Now that we have ascertained that it is a suitable pestilence, let's go on to see how we will take it to the humans." He turned and looked at Itoff for support.

Itoff was compelled to nod encouragingly.

"Rats are of no use in this case because humans would have nothing to do with them. We will rather use animals that are not repugnant to humans such as monkeys."

"Are you suggesting that these depraved earthlings are now copulating with monkeys?" Funkuin who had been silent for all this while stepped in.

"Some starved young bucks in those Asian, African and South American jungles probably try their luck with the primates once in a while," offered a bald-headed bloke who was sitting next to Funkuin.

"Nothing like that," said Fulumfuchong. "You blighters seem to have dirty minds. Monkeys are found all over in laboratories, zoos and circuses. Besides, monkey meat is a delicacy on earth."

"But the interaction between monkeys and humans is very limited" Funkuin pointed out.

"Maybe" admitted Fulumfuchong "But that is just the starting point. Unlike your previous ideas that failed woefully we have not concentrated only on one aspect. The monkeys will serve as a source of one of the dangerous strains. It will spread widely because of the constant movement by air, land and sea."

"That is okay. Next aspect," ordered Itoff.

"Since there are very few wild monkeys in America and the developed world that could be hunted and eaten, we will use something far better than the neutron bomb approach."

"You must be joking," put in Funkuin.

"I have never felt less like joking in my life. The idea is that we are borrowing a little from here and there. Some computer laboratories on earth spend a lot of money and time on research just to create a computer virus. When the virus spreads, they create an antidote and sell it. We intend to exploit this strategy. This time, our agents will not pass through secretaries to sneak formulae into research offices. They will corner a few hungry capitalists who have the greedy intention of becoming richer than Croesus. These would be chaps involved in the pharmaceutical sector. They will hand over to them the formula for creating this new deadly disease in their laboratories, and they will spread the disease rapidly."

"I am sure all those your bumbling spies would be apprehended before the plant the first formula," Funkuin was not about to be defeated easily.

"No problem about that," retorted Fulumfuchong. "All our spies will be re-educated and given new names. They will all be called Innocent."

"Why would they all want to answer to a name like that?" This time, it was another female.

"That is for protection. Humans have developed an instrument they call a lie detector. When spies are apprehended, they use this gadget to find out whether they are speaking the truth or not. If any of our spies falls into the hands of the KGB, the FBI or any of those secret police agencies, they will end all their statements by insisting that they are innocent. That will confuse the lie detector because they will be telling the truth by saying that they are called Innocent.

"Why do you think human capitalists will agree to use this new disease to destroy their own world?" The question came from a squat fellow who felt he should also participate.

"They will be lured into this with a promise that they will eventually be given the formula for the vaccine and the cure when the disease starts raging. All the greedy capitalists would go for that."

"How do you plan to succeed, then, if you plan to give them antidotes?"

"We are not that stupid. We will only use the idea to lure them into spreading the disease. After that we will instead fight any attempts on their part to develop antidotes."

"Humans are very smart and innovative. What makes you think that within this long period that the disease will take to nail them decisively, they would not have found a cure?" asked Itoff

Fulumfuchong looked round confidently and replied.

"Our virus is not as common as the others. In fact the reason why it takes a longer time to kill is because it has a system of protecting itself. We have designed it such that it mutates into a new form each time an effective weapon is found to destroy it, and each new form takes a different type of weapon to destroy. I tell you, the humans will never find any solution for its destruction until it has wiped out the whole world."

"What of distant places from America like Russia?" This question came from a cross eyed female.

"It takes just one carrier of the disease to travel from America to Tasmania, to Ulan Bator or to Punta Arenas and have fun with a local unsuspecting belle, maybe a sex worker. In a few days she would have had sex with other men, husbands, students, fiancés, etc. In a year, if we consider the Malthusian implication of geometric proportion, we can imagine the outcome in a year or two."

At last applause came from three academics as a cute damsel commented:

"You can imagine the rate in highly promiscuous areas like Bangkok, Douala or Lagos." She had risen very fast in status, thanks to a very influential mother.

"Sure!" said Fulumfuchong. "And we will also send down some Mungongoh beauties to help push the spread of the pestilence faster and further."

"That requires an explanation," said Itoff. "Or are you planning to get our women infected too?"

"The pretty faces that we will send down face no risk. They shall spread the disease, but shall be well protected; the pestilence will not penetrate their systems."

"If I understand well, your plan involves giving our young girls out for those depraved earthlings to have sex with," said Funkuin in a bid to rally support against the idea.

"Look who is talking," replied Fulumfuchong. "Your foolish idea of bombs involved the agent Nyamfuka to go sleeping with secretaries on earth. What is the difference with this one, or is it because it concerns women?"

Funkuin was quiet, but still searching for a flaw in the whole thing. She finally landed on one.

"Your idea may be quite good, and sound very effective. But there are very many sexually active persons who are not heterosexuals. I am talking about homosexuals in this case. Take some of those priests in America and elsewhere, for example, whose favourites are mass boys, or some of those great musicians who prefer to be slept with by other men. Homosexuals are quite many and have to be considered."

"Remember, Madam," replied Fulumfuchong, "We are talking about sexually transmitted diseases and have not limited them to heterosexuals. Even then, we have bisexuals who could always catch the disease from the heterosexuals and transmit it to the homosexuals. Besides, the concept of our virus from the lab is such that it will pass through drug addicts as they share needles and these could either be heterosexuals or homosexuals. Nobody is spared."

"I am still a bit doubtful about this idea of yours," the cross eyed female said "What of the thousands of women locked up in harems or women in far away igloos and such remote areas?"

"Women in harems belong to lecherous sheiks who still stray out when ever they have the opportunity. They also keep marrying new wives, who could bring along the disease. As for women in the remote areas, there are constant visits from horny journalists, researchers, tax officers, visiting clergymen, you name it. I assure you again, nobody can be spared."

"Any more worries or questions?" asked Itoff in a bid to close the debate.

Itoff was always hasty in closing debates over any idea developed by him or one of his close assistants. He however allowed debates to last for as long as possible when it concerned others, especially chaps like Fulumfuchong that he personally disliked. This is why he had let this one go n for as long as it had.

Funkuin would not let go.

"I am not really seeing all the earthlings dying. Whatever happens, a few of them will survive.".

"That is very true and that is just what we want. There are certain things on earth that earthlings know best how to handle. Wipe all of them out and we might get stuck somewhere. What we want is to weaken them to such a point where we could then stroll in and take over without much resistance. We will easily subdue the few remaining weaklings. You should note that every active human is interested in sex, either as a heterosexual, a bisexual or a homosexual. Why, some of them have been known to use dogs and other animals for sexual gratification. What we will therefore be left to deal with would be the weak, the very shy and the very reserved. They are very few, you know."

Funkuin was unrelenting.

"The few humans that we accommodate may soon grow one day to be as formidable as the Israelites, and take back the world some day."

"No problem," replied Fulumfuchong, still full of confidence. "They will not procreate. We will render all of them impotent. You think we would leave those human Romeos to go prancing around? Some of you females would end up with their children."

There was a cocktail of laughter, ranging from high pitched nasal solos to deep guttural baritones.

"What do you take us females for?" shrieked Funkuin. "I am sure you simply want to disguise the fact that your plan has allowed for a few human females to be taken over so that you go wagging your tails."

"Hold it!" yelled Itoff. "This is not one of those human parliaments."

When the idea was taken to King Awobua by Mobuh, all questions and answers that came up in the academy of toughs were presented for his appraisal. He enjoyed the exchange and turned to Mobuh

"I don't remember that any discussion on any idea has been as exhaustive as this."

"It is because everybody wanted to be sure it was a winner before accepting that it should be brought to you." replied Mobuh. I had made it clear to them that you have tolerated enough failures already and will not be blamed for any rash reaction if the next idea fails.

"And you think this one will work?"

"From every indication, Sir" replied Mobuh, happy that the atmosphere was not that tense.

"But I wonder whether I can wait for all this while," the king said thoughtfully.

"You see sir, since this is a concrete and sure idea that will eliminate the earthlings; we had better put it in process, then call for other ideas that can accelerate the process."

"You think so?"

"Yes sir, we can call for more ideas; although it will cost a little bit more, it will beef up what we have. The advantage we have is that we don't have short lives like humans. With our average life span of ten thousand years, one year is a short period for us."

"That is true," said King Awobua, more satisfied. He took a swig of the strange brew in front of him and grimaced.

The king's usual brew was *mukal*, but it had been recommended by his medics that he should switch to other drinks once in a while. This gave a lot of work to the kitchen staff, who had the task of coming up with a completely new brew fit for royal consumption. The fact that any form of poisoning would certainly be blamed on them made them extremely careful. After exhausting all their list of recipes fit for a king, they were compelled to improvise. With their expertise, they often surfaced with good stuff, but once in a while the result was repulsive. This was one of those days.

"May be we should forget about the medics and have you stick to your favourite *mukal*," suggested Mobuh quickly as he noticed that the stuff in front of the king was not appropriate for the royal palate.

"These guys are certainly plotting to make me mad," said the king, pouring the revolting stuff into a huge flower pot. "I will consider what you have just proposed"

"So we can go ahead with this new idea?" asked Mobuh.

"Yes, although I am wondering whether I should not mete out punishment for the past failures. I treat you rascals very well, pay you handsomely, yet I cannot have results. I want to be the king of the earth, not some small satellite close to the earth."

"You shall Sir, very soon, Sir" Mobuh was doing everything to please the king.

"Go and put this plan into action," ordered the king

"Yes Sir, immediately Sir," Mobuh rushed out of the

king's presence, preferring to be where he was considered boss. He was like the prime minister of Mungongoh and everybody else, apart from the king, trembled before him.

In his office, he buzzed for Fulumfuchong, who surfaced within fifteen minutes.

8

Fulumfuchong's ghastly idea was sneaked into the earth unnoticed. The first persons to be targeted were drug addicts who were always generous in sharing. Infected heroin and cocaine were sent down to earth and mixed up with the dope circulating in druggie circles. The first casualties easily transmitted the disease to others through the common use of needles. Since the anal mucous membrane of humans was more fragile than that of the vagina or the mouth, it was easy for transmission from infected persons to others to take place during homosexual intercourse.

However, after a short while, Fulumfuchong realized that homosexual activities were very limited and that infection would move faster through heterosexuals. The necessity to put his second plan into action became apparent. He was going to include heterosexual transmission especially through the oversexed and the sector in the earth's population that was most exposed to sexual activities. Flight crews of the biggest commercial airlines on earth were his first target, and it was quite an appropriate choice, given their exposure to beautiful females where ever their flight jobs took them to. The idea was to discreetly get them infected with the new pestilence, and this was transmitted through beautiful Mungongoh females who lured the targeted fellows into sex. The Mungongoh females themselves were in no danger as they had been protected before being sent down. Flying saucers that had brought them to earth immediately conveyed them back to Mungongoh immediately their job was done.

Back in Mungongoh, their protection was reinforced before they were sent down to the second targeted group.

This comprised popular actors who had all the female earthlings at their beck and call.

In Equatorial Africa, infected monkeys were introduced into the jungle. African hunters ate the contaminated meat, got contaminated themselves, and transmitted the disease through sexual intercourse with their partners. In Africa however, the devastation was not so great. The forest dwellers who ate the infected monkeys, had little access to women outside their tiny hamlets, and so the spread in that area was limited.

Heterosexuals proved even better transmitters than homosexuals, but it was only after a few big politicians got hit that it became apparent that something was wrong.

This was not the first time that Mungongoh had attempted to wipe out the human race from the surface of the earth through pestilence; but each had come with a specific name. At one time it was typhus. Then there was smallpox, followed by syphilis, malaria, tuberculosis, typhoid, and other diseases. This time, Fulumfuchong had left it to humans to put a tag on this new virulent disease. In the absence of a real name, therefore, the earthlings simply called it a syndrome.

Fulumfuchong seemed to have finally come up with just the right thing. The spread was remarkable. Even areas with sexually inhibited lifestyles were affected.

King Awobua summoned Mobuh to his inner sanctum and when he entered, the king beamed and offered him a glass of chilled *mukal*. A dwarf went over to the refrigerator, brought out a pitcher, and poured a glassful for Mobuh.

Mukal had always been the king's favourite drink and he had finally settled on it after Mobuh's advice. It had thus been reserved only for the king and everybody else banned from consuming it. The whole of Mungongoh had come to a conclusion that Kadji beer was good for them, so they did not quite miss the king's *mukal*.

"That boy Fulumfuchong," he boomed. "The guy is simply wonderful. I don't know why you have been wasting time with those other dumb scientists. This takes the cake."

"I am glad you are satisfied, Sir" replied Mobuh.

"Satisfied?" I am elated!"

The king pointed to the large screen in front of him.

"Just look at that" he said, "follow that news bulletin closely."

A chubby female was reading out figures of the alarming death from the disease they had dubbed 'Acquired Immune Deficiency Syndrome' simplified as AIDS.

"And despite the rate at which this devastation is taking place, the humans still seem to enjoy their depraved lifestyle. Look here," he pointed.

The scene had switched over to Bangkok, where tourists were having fun in some popular hotels with beautiful Thai girls.

After a hearty guffaw, the king said "while the men are having a swell time with those beautiful Thai girls, their old ladies would not be left behind. Thai Ladyboys are making a fortune out of them".

The king switched over to Mombassa where gigolos, wearing tight trousers to emphasize the size of their manhood, were moving temptingly around some female tourists from Sweden and Germany. Then a scene in Manila came up with child prostitutes haggling over prices with some horny old men. There was still more. The next scene showed soldiers in some African country, Cameroon or Togo, telling young village girls that a soldier does not eat bananas with the skin on, in a bid to lure them into unprotected sex.

"That is wonderful, Sir" said Mobuh.

"At least I am now assured that one day I will become King of the earth, not some small rocky satellite of Mars." He turned to Mobuh.

"You would like to become a real prime minister, wouldn't you?"

"Of course, Sir, that is, if it is your royal wish."

The King picked up a remote control and switched to another earth observatory. His favourite pastime was to observe the earth, as his most fervent passion was to become the king of this vast domain. He was thoroughly enjoying the attachment of the earthlings to sex, which was proof that Fulumfuchong's virus would work well. Sex seemed to be the central interest of the earthlings, heterosexuals or homosexuals. The next scene he landed on proved that.

The scene was bright and loud. It was actually an international gay conference holding in Adelaide in Australia. The hall was colourfully decorated and the walls were covered with suggestive and explicit posters promoting gay activities and declaring the rights of gay people.

The audience was a motley crowd, ranging from well dressed ladies and gentlemen to youths wearing dresses and shirts of shouting and revolting colours. Some of the youths wore very tight trousers and spotted weird hairdos. There were men and women of the cloth mixed inside the crowd and some of them had boldly come in their cassocks and habits The Master of Ceremonies was a robust, red-faced Swede who towered over the Anglican Bishop that he was about to introduce to the crowd.

"Ladies and Gentlemen, fellow gay colleagues, I welcome you to this great international conference of Adelaide. You will make yourselves comfortable and listen to powerful speeches from inspired men and women. We have made every arrangement to provide for leisure and fun during intervals. The toilets are clean and ready for those smart fellows who are lucky enough to convince a neighbour to accept a quickie. The bloke smiled mischievously and continued, "I am introducing to you Bishop Winterbottom. He will tell us a lot about homosexuality and Christianity."

There was a lot of clapping as he stepped aside and allowed the bishop to take over the microphone. The bishop looked like something obtained from crossing a Pekinese with a Tasmanian devil.

"Fellow homosexuals and lesbians," the high priest shouted as he came on, "these words simply describe our sexual orientation. Yes, instead of going for the opposite sex, we are rather attracted to members of our own sex. Males prefer males and females prefer females. Our situation is thus termed abnormal by the so-called normal persons. But I don't think we are abnormal. Is there anything wrong with us?"

"No!" the audience shouted back.

"True," said the bishop. "Abnormal persons are those who are impotent or totally frigid. But we are hot and active. In fact hotter than most heterosexuals."

He removed a large silk handkerchief from his pocket and wiped his face and nose.

"God has his way with everything. He made all humans and animals to enjoy sex, and to enjoy it each in his or her way. Yes, God decided that humans could enjoy sex in various ways. He made us to enjoy sex this way. Who is there then to question the way we enjoy sex, and even have the audacity to declare that it is sinful?"

The response was thunderous

"I am telling you all here that most Christian authorities exaggerate. Yes, I am a bishop of the Anglican Church and I know what I am talking about. It was quite a hard struggle to make me bishop. Christian authorities would prefer a notoriously promiscuous bishop or priest to a faithful, humble and happily married homosexual."

There was another thunderous round of applause.

"In the Bible, we read about the sin of Onan. That is where the bible openly condemns a sexual act and it involved *coitus interruptus*. On the other hand, when homosexual practices in Sodom and Gomorra were mentioned in the Bible, homosexuality in itself was not labelled as a sin. What was sinful was the act of soliciting or trying to force the strangers into having unlawful sex. In short, God does not condemn homosexuality anywhere."

The speaker stopped to appreciate the reaction from the crowd, smiled and continued.

"God made sex strictly for procreation in some animals. Others like cocks, however enjoy it as often as they feel like it. In humans, sex is not only meant for procreation. It is also meant to bring persons closer together. Where sex is absent, an active couple splits immediately. No active woman remains faithful to a totally impotent man. She must look for sexual satisfaction somewhere out of the relationship. The importance of sex in the life of a couple or persons who love themselves and want to remain faithful to each other is therefore quite evident. Now, if partners faced with an impotent husband are bound to cheat in order to have sexual satisfaction, it means that single persons also need and look for sexual satisfaction. We have thus established that God made sex an important part of life, whether you are married or not. Sex is mainly to be enjoyed, therefore. Procreation simply comes after. During sex, heterosexuals use different orifices apart from the one they claim was provided by God for such encounters. Where, then, have we homosexuals gone wrong? We use the tongue just like them and different orifices just like them. We use sex to love each other and stay together. It is true we cannot procreate this way, but we have established the fact that God's primary intention for creating sex was to give his children something they would like and something that would keep them together. Not every couple must have children."

Everybody in the hall agreed with him and showed it fully. He was not about to stop.

"If any of you has read this book known as the Da Vinci Code, you would have found mentioned therein that our great Lord Jesus Christ, whom we consider to be God, had a child with Mary Magdalene. All of us sitting inside here are aware of the fact that the Holy Grail is understood to be the cup that Jesus used during the Last Supper. This book insists that the Holy Girl, I mean Grail, is the child that Jesus Christ had with Mary Magdalene. This book wants to portray Christ as an active heterosexual. However, a closer look into writings concerning the life of Christ, shows that they dwell on a close attachment between him and the apostle, John. Their relationship appeared to have been so close that there could have been a sexual aspect to it. None of us today lived at that time, but the possibility that our great Lord and Christ might have had a homosexual relationship in his day justifies our inclination to homosexuality."

In their heyday, a combination of Mick Jagger and the Rolling Stones, and Michael Jackson would never have received such a standing ovation. There was a lot of hugging and kissing, hats and caps tossed into the air, continuous hand clapping and shouts for an encore.

."Now, we have established that sex is important in the lives of all humans and can be enjoyed as heterosexuals or homosexuals. What we need to establish now is marriage. In the Holy Bible, Jesus Christ is quite right when he lists adultery among the most grievous crimes on earth. This gives the impression that if one partner was caught sexually cheating on the other, even divorce could be accepted as the possible step to be taken by the aggrieved party. It should be noted that Jesus did not mention the incapacity to reproduce as a sin. It is indicative that all God-fearing governments and churches must allow marriage between homosexuals who love each other. I am sure we would make better couples and prove more faithful to our partners. They are forcing us to live in sin, although our sin of fornication is less repulsive than that of adultery."

The king had been beaming with satisfaction through out this scene and still grinning very broadly, he switched to another scene. The new scene was a laboratory where scientists were struggling to discover vaccines that could fight off the new virus. He could see disappointment in the eyes of the scientists as they seemed to be making no headway.

King Awobua laughed happily, stamping his feet on the floor. Even the dwarfs seemed to be happy.

Life went on normally in Mungongoh as AIDS ravaged the earth. Although the initial intention of spreading AIDS in Sub-Saharan Africa through primates had failed, the virus had been brought in from America and spread widely. The toll in Africa was already alarming. As Fulumfuchong had mentioned during the defence of his idea, the virus could mutate easily and protect itself from vaccines and cures that were discovered. Most countries on earth were already spending a fortune on AIDS research without any success. Mungongoh agents on earth brought in constant news of such failed attempts to develop a cure or a vaccine. The agents also had the task of nipping in the bud any fledgling signs of success.

Most persons on earth initially blamed the ravaging pestilence on homosexuals. They claimed that it was God's punishment to those who were practicing sex the wrong way. This was based on the fact transmission had initially been limited to homosexual activities. At that time, heterosexuals were still spared and did know that their turn was coming. The disease thus exposed and embarrassed many homosexuals in high places who had kept their sexual inclinations a well-guarded secret. It was when the pestilence mutated to a form which could be easily transmitted heterosexually and when a new heterosexual strain was introduced through beautiful Mungongoh girls, that the theory of punishment for homosexuals was jettisoned.

The situation on earth remained confused as eminent statesmen, prominent artists and writers, respected members of the clergy and innocent children kept dying of the pestilence without a real name. Several theories developed as to the origin and the cause of the pestilence. While the Vatican simply called on all Christians to pray and ask for God's help, Pentecostal churches went further. They declared that God had been pushed too far by the hideous sins people on earth were committing. They thus attributed the syndrome, as it was known on earth, to some divine warning of worse things to come. Some pastors even claimed that through deliverance sessions, they could rid AIDS victims of the affliction. Of course, no actual healings were ever recorded, but they succeeded in luring away several wealthy people from regular Christian churches.

Apart from divine punishment other theories sought to explain the source of the pestilence. It was claimed that America had been alarmed by the population explosion in Third World countries that compelled many of them to escape from their impoverished and over populated countries and crowd into America. The strange disease had been developed in some lab, with the purpose of planting it in any Third World countries where the population was going out of control. The virus had escaped prematurely and was now proving its effectiveness. How it came to be sexually transmitted was not quite explained by this theory.

However, not everybody looked at AIDS negatively. A group of female activists developed a television program on the advantages of AIDS. In this program they used four main points to explain how AIDS was going to put an end to sexual decadence in the world and bring husband and wife even closer.

The first point they dwelt on was the fact that AIDS was going to discourage early sexual activities among the youth. Their daughters would thus be frightened from giving in to boys and sugar daddies prematurely. The second point stated that brothels and havens of sex workers would disappear as husbands would hurry home to the safety of their wives. The third point held that AIDS would scare many husbands away from having extramarital affairs with friends and relatives of their wives, while the fourth point considered the possibility of polygamy ceasing to exist in Africa and some Arab countries because of the fear of AIDS.

There were still many who believed that AIDS did not actually exist and was rather a scare that had been developed to discourage sex. It was not quite clear who had developed the scare, however.

For two years, the innocent and the promiscuous were dying on earth. Despite all efforts, no cure had been discovered. Neither was there a vaccine. Ten great footballers, three presidents and hundreds of ministers had died. However, all was not yet lost. In the absence of a cure, a few drugs had been discovered that could prolong the life of an afflicted person. There were food supplements that added more vitality to an AIDS-stricken person and made him look quite normal.

On the other hand, since the people of the earth could not live without sex and still remained very promiscuous, teenage girls indulged in early sex even more than before. Brothels and sex workers thrived on and polygamy remained a popular form of marriage among many Africans and Arabs. Our female activists were now quite disappointed. However, preventive measures were introduced. The use of the condom in sex was reinforced and lots of seminars on AIDS and AIDS prevention were organized. More and more money was being pumped into AIDS research and better options of drugs for maintenance were developed.

The IRDI was already concentrated on an idea that seemed to be succeeding well, so most of its members were no longer working on new ideas. They were busy going about their various extracurricular duties although at the same time, they were all very anxious to see the outcome of Fulumfuchong's devastating idea.

9

At the end of five years however, King Awobua wanted an analysis of the real situation and how long it was going to take for the earth to be completely subdued. Although the dead toll from AIDS was still high, the people were not dying fast enough. Besides, there was still a high birth rate in many parts of the earth.

Mobuh therefore summoned a meeting with Itoff and all his super brains.

"Our king has been very patient so far despite the rather prolonged trend of things." This opening remark was received with some apprehension.

"Yes, he thinks we are moving towards our ultimate goal of wiping out those hopeless humans from the surface of the earth, so that we can make better use of their productive soil, but the pace is not fast enough. Remember, it was expected that this pestilence will take just one year to kill the afflicted person. Now, the earthlings are containing somehow and it takes longer to kill."

There was complete silence in the room.

"So!" continued Mobuh, "the King wants us to put our heads together and come up with an assessment of the degree of success and what, if anything, may be delaying us from getting to the end. We need to know how things are going on and to determine whether we need to put in more steam or allow things go on as they are. The King is certain that we failed in our earlier attempts because you blighters omitted the aspect of monitoring, evaluation or assessment, a thing you might have simply copied from the earthlings."

"Now, look at this other scene."

The scene came up and young girls of twelve and thirteen years were unrolling condoms onto wooden phalluses in a classroom. As some shock was expressed, Funkuin quickly moved the scene to a condom shop in a university hostel in America, where the old sales woman was wanting to know from the young Finnish girl whether the man she wanted to use the condom with was Black, Hispanic, Arab, Asian or Europeans, so she could determine the size of the condom to sell to her. The laughter that erupted made Funkuin conclude that she needed another more convincing scene. She then switched to another scene where some young rascals were deconstructing the Pope's homily against the use of condoms

"What do you really intend to show?" questioned Itoff.

"It is quite simple," replied Funkuin

"All these scenes show an effective preventive measure that the humans will use against your pestilence. You can see that even the mighty Pope himself is finding it extremely difficult to convince earthlings to give up the condom."

"But when did this condom idea come up?"

"It has always been on earth and somebody did not think of it when developing his wonderful idea which the earthlings now call AIDS," said Funkuin.

Fulumfuchong thought it was time for him to step in.

"The condom is proof of the high level of promiscuity on earth. It was developed to prevent early pregnancies in teenage children, and the birth of illegitimate children in the case of adultery."

"But its use is now being adjusted to prevent the transmission of AIDS. You can see how the doctrine of Papal infallibility is being challenged just because he preaches against the use of condoms. I tell you condoms as a means of protecting AIDS is catching up with your disease." Funkuin smirked in triumph.

"What she is saying is hogwash," Fulumfuchong assured the others. "Condoms are known to burst frequently. Besides, many men and women do not like them. Many African women who assume that they are respectable feel insulted if a man brings out a condom when they are about to have sex. As for the elderly men, many of them have weak erections and the penis tends to droop when they are struggling to put on a condom. Such men often go straight, that is to say, have sex without a condom, but they look so responsible that they are always trusted by the women."

Fulumfuchong glared at Funkuin and continued.

"Anyway we are counting more on the high infidelity rate among the humans. A man has unprotected sex with his wife and girlfriends. He uses a condom only when he strays out of this small group. The wife equally has unprotected sex with her boyfriend or boyfriends. The girlfriends have fiancés or other trusted men with whom they indulge in unprotected sex. The chain is long and makes it certain that the virus will spread rapidly."

"Any other worry?" asked Itoff

"We are all convinced, said a young, cute female scientist called Yivissi. It is clear that it is a well studied idea, with no stone left unturned. Let's give it more time.

"Okay then, any contrary opinion?"

Even Funkuin remained mute.

"All right," concluded Mobuh

"This time, Fulumfuchong will come with me to King Awobua to convince him to be a bit more patient."

The king received them the next day in the afternoon. As they went in, he lifted a glass of green wine which he had placed on the flat bald pate of a middle aged dwarf kneeling by his side, took a swift swig and pointed at Fulumfuchong with the glass.

"Is that the geezer who came up with this supper idea about this pestilence which the humans now call AIDS?"

"Yes sir" said Fulumfuchong bowing to the king

"And how many more centuries do we have to wait for your idea to work fully, a lifetime?"

Unlike humans who hardly live up to a century, the people of Mungongoh have an average life span of ten centuries. King Awobua was middle aged, about six hundred years old, while the beefy Mobuh was older, having clocked close to eight centuries.

"The problem is that humans seem to have a way out of everything Sir, but this time we have tied the knot quite well. It may take a bit of time but eventually the earthlings will be wiped out, Sir."

"I want results," replied the king. "That is the only reason why I will spare you for now. I will give you five more years. During those years you must work hard, or else you know where you will end up."

Fulumfuchong left the king's presence quite shaken. He had not expected the king to hug him happily and pour praises on him, but neither was he expecting a short time limit and the promise of a tragic end. Back in Mobuh's office, he was quick to bring up the topic.

"The king did not mean what he said, did he?"

"Mean what?"

"The deadline and the promise of an agonizing death in case we don't meet the deadline."

"The king is always very serious, so if you don't accomplish his aims, better prepare to be gobbled up by ferocious lions. Anyway, I hear it is less excruciating than the noose of a hangman."

Fulumfuchong shuddered. Even his loose folds seemed to quiver along.

Mobuh went ahead without seeming to notice anything.

"King Awobua is a very patient and tolerant person, but you bozos always want to push him to the wall. Anyway, to make sure that you are not transformed into steak for feline consumption, I will call another meeting of the institute of ideas. Maybe one or more of the academicians will come up with other ideas that will beef up this one of a sexually transmitted pestilence that is already failing."

10

The next gathering of academicians came as a relief to Fulumfuchong, although it was rather heated. After a brief introduction from Mobuh, the floor was thrown open for contributions. Mobuh had deliberately omitted the royal threat to feed people to lions and simply gave the academicians to understand that it was necessary to beef up the current idea to guarantee success.

"I had sensed right from the beginning that this idea of a sexually transmitted disease was of no good," said Funkuin smugly.

"Nobody has said that it has failed," defended Fulumfuchong. "We are simply looking for ways of adding more flesh to it."

"Why would such an impeccable idea, as you described it, need beefing up? Has it developed engine trouble?" Funkuin was having a good time.

"Now, silence you two!" Mobuh growled. "This is a serious meeting, not meant for bickering and useless exchanges. I want only constructive contributions to this issue."

"What I would suggest," said Itoff is that we attack on all fronts. Our problem is that we always use only one idea at a time, and the idea always ends up being neutralised by those cursed earthlings."

"What do you propose, then?" asked Mobuh

"Let us add more pestilences. Fill the whole world with pestilences and they will not be able to cope," replied Itoff.

"He is quite right," contributed Funkuin. "We could even add a dose of harmful bombs for good measure."

"You and your dashed harmless bombs," mocked Fulumfuchong.

"Let's look at what Itoff has proposed," announced Mobuh. "I actually think it is good."

"Okay," said the youngish cute female, Yivissi. "We should start by working on the strain of the virus that Fulumfuchong passed through African monkeys without much success. I will add to this another more devastating strain known as Ebola. The Ebola virus will spread faster and wreak more havoc."

"I hope you are sure of what you are saying," Mobuh said hopefully. "Fulumfuchong, take note of what she has said. We should try it."

"Anything transmitted through monkeys will not go far. Why don't we try something that is often in close contact with the earthlings?" a professor of animal sciences contributed. "I give you the mad cow disease."

"What is that supposed to be?" enquired Funkuin.

"It is something we developed in the lab. It is a pestilence that we can pass through cows, an animal that constitutes the main source of animal proteins for all earthlings."

"Fulumfuchong, record that one too. It sounds formidable," ordered Mobuh. "Any other bright idea?"

Another professor of animal biology had been carrying out destructive research. "All the ideas that have been proposed are good but not good enough. I see serious limitations in all of them."

"Speak up, then!" shouted Mobuh

"The animals proposed will not have access to human beings far and wide. Besides, they can be easily isolated and destroyed. Let us try something else."

"And what, may I ask?" Itoff was afraid that other persons might take the credit for his idea.

"Birds. Fowls. These creatures are found in the wild all over and in virtually all animal farms. They are found in virtually all villages in the world. Another thing that makes them the most efficient carriers of pestilence is the fact that they have migratory tendencies. Many bird species travel far and mingle with domestic birds. They are also game. Actually, if birds had been used for the Fire plague, the idea would have certainly been highly successful."

"You have not quite landed," Itoff pointed out.

"What I have been working on is the bird flu. It will not fail us."

"But we tried a flu before and eventually gave it up" protested Itoff.

A rotund fellow with bulging eyes butted in: "Flues could be very strong and effective. The influenza we sent down in 1918-1919, which the earthlings dubbed Spanish flu, might have failed in the end, but during the brief period, it was more devastating than Fulumfuchong's AIDS has proven so far. It rapidly spread from America north to the Eskimos, south to Asuncion and far off in the east to Samoa. We succeeded in striking down about fifty million earthlings in the prime of their lives. It is clear that the flu is the most effective pestilence to use in ridding the earth of humans. The problem with our first attempt in 1918 was that we relied on the virus to spread naturally from person to person in respiratory secretions expelled into the immediate environment by talking, sneezing and coughing. We had overlooked the use of an appropriate animal host through which we could sustain the spread of the pestilence. Birds could be a good animal host but I prefer pigs as my transmitters."

Hilarious laughter erupted from Itoff and a group of academicians.

"Pigs!" Itoff chuckled. "What an absurd animal. Why would pigs work when half the world would not touch them?"

"Pork" said the rotund guy, unperturbed, "is consumed much more than you think. The Russians and Slavs consume a lot of lard. Bacon is very popular all over Europe and America. In Latin America, Africa, China and much of Asia, Australia, and the Pacific islands, roast pork is a delicacy. Even within Arab countries, there are Christian or pagan populations that consume pork. Meanwhile, a pig is much more expensive than a chicken, so pig keepers will hesitate very much to dispose of an infected pig. They would prefer to take the risk and sneak the dead animal carcasses into meat considered as safe to eat.

"Well then," declared Mobuh, let us add bird and swine flu to our collection.

Fulumfuchong scribbled down the new addition.

"Should we leave it at that?" asked Mobuh

After a moment's silence, another scientist chirped.

"In talking about the usefulness of animals in our program to destroy the earth, we have left out sheep and goats. I have already succeeded in developing the foot and mouth disease in sheep and hope very soon to make its devastating effect extend to humans."

"How soon will that be?" enquired Itoff.

"I can't really say."

"Then we should not bother about it." This was the general conclusion that came as if in a chorus.

Itoff cleared his throat loudly as a way of attracting every body's attention.

"I am sure we have collected quite a number of solid ideas which can help to accelerate the present idea that now holds sway and bring the destruction of the earth to a hasty conclusion. All of us here want to serve our king in the best way, and see him fully satisfied. You would agree with me that there is nothing he would want better than becoming a powerful monarch of the earth. I am sure all of you present here would also feel great at being part of the new grand world."

The laboratories in Mungongoh went into full swing. Small doses of the various pestilences that had been agreed upon were produced or improved upon and sent down to the earth. Mungongoh agents were quite busy coming and going. For two whole years, the bustle was remarkable and quite a considerable sum of *kuo* was spent. Reports from the royal treasury showed that the kingdom would soon go bankrupt at that pace. In panic the king asked for Ngess, dismissing every attempt by Mobuh to keep Ngess at bay and continue with the costly idea that was being implemented.

"Go and bring him here immediately!" the king barked.

Mobuh turned on his communication system and gave orders. "Drop anything you are doing and come to the palace immediately."

Ngess was at the dentist's, having his teeth checked.

"In an hour's time sir, I am fully occupied right now." he pleaded.

"The lions will soon be occupied with your bones if you don't make it snappy!" shouted Mobuh.

Ngess pushed aside the dentist's drill stood up and rushed out of the dentistry.

The surprised dentist rushed after him shouting for payment.

Mobuh's wrist phone buzzed and Ngess came on.

"I am on my way sir, as soon as I settle the dentist's bill."

"You are not going to waste a minute settling bills. Drop everything and fly."

Ngess excused himself to the confused dentist and actually flew.

"My dear man," said the king when Ngess was ushered in, "it looks as if you are the only one left in this kingdom who has his head screwed on the right way."

"I am much obliged, Sir," Ngess said, bowing.

"What has been going on in Mungongoh is no secret to anybody. I am sure you are quite aware of our reinforced offensive on the earth, and the fact that it does not seem to be working as we imagined." The king was making every effort to be calm. He had decided that the only way to get Ngess to speak freely would be to make him as relaxed as possible.

"I am aware of everything, Sir," said Ngess, and he continued courageously, "it is just that nobody ever seeks the opinion of a simple man like me, when there are big professors spilling out lofty ideas from their large brains."

"You should be more respectful," warned Mobuh

"Let him be." the king was doing everything to keep Ngess at ease. "So, what do you think of all this?"

"Although it was a great strategy and all the ideas are solid, the whole thing was poorly coordinated."

"What rubbish!" interjected Mobuh, who had been part of the coordination. "The best professors of the land were working on the strategy."

"That is just the problem" replied Ngess calmly. The king was actually succeeding in putting him at ease. "Each big brain thought his idea was the best and tried to put it ahead while avoiding promoting the others, even if he could."

"Can you explain this more clearly?" asked the king.

"Each pestilence was introduced in small doses in an area chosen by its initiator, and many of them are not experts on earth strategy. Before the pestilence spreads anywhere, countermeasures are already in place. If you start any pestilence and want it to be effective, tackle America and Europe at once, where the best labs are located."

"The mad cow was introduced in Europe," Mobuh pointed out.

"True, but most of the Europeans have no access to cows. Cows are kept far off in farms and many Europeans prefer chicken and fish. Before the disease could get to America, serious defences had been put up."

"You are saying that we should give up this last strategy as lost?" King Awobua asked sadly.

"It will never work sir. It will go on killing humans, no doubt, but not to the extent that will result in the elimination of the human race. They have to come up with something else."

"Thank you, you may leave" the king said, despondent.

11

King Awobua became sad. He looked more like a lover boy who had just lost his young sweetheart. He refused to receive any of his subjects, even Mobuh, for one full month. During this period, he had neither eaten nor drunk anything, and he had destroyed two dozen dwarfs. On the other hand, it was the best time the royal lions had ever had. Apart from twenty four dwarfs, ten scientists had been transformed into choice meals for them. Mobuh himself had been spared only because King Awobua considered him virtually irreplaceable. Mobuh had even succeeded in saving the lives of a few favourites of his like Itoff, by explaining to the king that tough brains would always be needed if the ultimate goal of occupying the earth would ever be achieved. However, Mobuh still dreaded every summon he received from the king.

He was thus very disturbed when the king himself strode into his office, a thing that had never happened.

Mobuh was in the process of gobbling some fried dung beetles, a snack that his wife often packaged and put in his briefcase. He jumped up hastily, overturning the silver plate from which he had been feeding on his special delicacy.

"Sit down," commanded the king

Mobuh's ample backside regained his chair but there was still a lot of consternation on his face.

"Is there any problem sir?" he asked, fearing the worst.

"Has there ever been any time on this blasted planet without problems?" roared the king. He looked now like an ogre whose last hope of getting a wife has been ruined by a nasty goblin.

"How can every thing go right when the righteous king is served by a host of incompetent subjects? You should be ashamed of yourselves. Imagine how a father would feel if all his children kept coming last in class."

"We have been doing our best sir; it is just that those earthlings too are very smart. They don't have several rulers for nothing."

"And what do you mean by that?" Enquired Awobua

"You see sir, unlike us with only one monarch; they have emperors, kings, pharaohs, presidents, sultans, caliphs, Kabakas, Asantehenes, Fons, you name them. All these heads together impose a kind of leadership that compels the people to surface with an expert solution at one time or another to any crisis situation."

"You want to call me incompetent, to put the blame rather on me?" asked king Awobua in a dangerously quiet voice.

Mobuh was sweating all over.

"Certainly not, Sir. You are more powerful than all of them. I will handle these stupid academicians of IRDI. They need to think harder."

"You better do. I am giving the last chance. In fact, what I came here to say is that I want an idea now that will not fail. If it does, I will clear all of you off the surface of Mungongoh and have my dwarfs as my subjects. I am sure those dwarfs will come up with better ideas if encouraged."

Mobuh imagined himself his flabby wife and plump offspring, all being torn to shreds by ferocious beasts.

"But sir, you can't have dwarfs for subjects, they are all retarded."

"Who says I won't prefer them to blokes like you who cannot surface with a single solid plan? I'd rather have my dumb dwarfs instead of flashy scientists who raise my hopes with flashy ideas just to dash them the next minute."

"This time they will surpass themselves, I promise." Mobuh had to say anything for the king to leave and give him some breathing space.

King Awobua's departure from Mobuh's office left the chief minister breathless. He rang for professor Itoff immediately.

"We are in serious trouble," he announced as Itoff came in. "We need something that will really work or the king will do something unthinkable."

As Itoff remained speechless in surprise, Mobuh continued.

"The king threatens to replace us with the dwarfs."

"You don't mean it?"

"Imagine a dwarf replacing me as chief minister and occupying this office," Mobuh clucked.

Itoff had still not found words.

"Itoff, you could then easily end up in the jaws of a lion or as a punching bag for the king."

At last, Itoff had something to say.

"But we have to stop him," said Itoff with much desperation.

"That is true, but we can only do that by coming up with an idea that works."

12

The next meeting of the institute of ideas was chaired by Mobuh himself. He had given two weeks for all the scientists to prepare and bring their ideas to that meeting. The prize for the sharpest idea would be Itoff's position, which was much coveted.

When the meeting started, several scientists came up with ideas that they declared would work perfectly well, but which were quickly dismissed. The various ideas already used were brought up again with modifications, but after serious discussion, these were abandoned. For three days, the meeting produced no acceptable idea and Mobuh was desperate.

On the forth day however some hope surfaced when the young female academician Yivissi took the floor.

"We have exhausted our stock of ideas it seems, using pestilences, animals, bombs, and whatnot. I believe we should now try something new, their God."

"We destroy the earth using their God?" Mobuh asked incredulously. "But they worship him. They believe in him and call him big names. How would such a god hurt anybody?"

"He would," replied Yivissi with confidence. "Although earthlings call him all those lovely names, he can be very angry and destructive. He has been known to wreak havoc in the past and destroy earthlings when ever they stretched his patience too far. In fact, at times, when we try some of our ideas on earth, the humans believe that it is vengeance or punishment from their God who must have run amok with anger. Do you know that in their holy book called the Bible, there are many destructive things such as floods, fires and pestilences that are blamed on this God? In that same book there are several other occasions where in anger he had struck viciously, destroying cities like Sodom and Gomorrah for simply practicing homosexuality, which is a common sexual practice today. In one famous case, he even struck down the couple, Ananias and Saphira simply because they held back a little bit of money from the sale of their own property instead of handing all of it over to the Apostles."

Itoff looked at Mobuh and smiled

"The young lady seems to be on the right track sir; let her continue."

Yivissi continued.

"Although this book is believed to have been written by a few blokes who lived at a time when language was virtually unwritten, the earthlings believe in it the way we are supposed to believe in every word that comes from the mouth of our king. This shows that they themselves are aware of the fact that their final damnation might come from their God than from anywhere else."

"But then, what can they do that would be so terrible that their God would want to destroy them? He is believed to have created them in the first place, and it is not easy to destroy your own creation." Mobuh wanted to clear off any scepticism. "Besides, they still say he is very understanding and forgiving."

In response, Yivissi switched on a large screen for all to see.

The scene was in a small country called Cameroon. Females were strolling around with blouses cut so that a large part of their breasts were exposed.

"You see," explained Yivissi "Clothes were fashioned so that women would be dressed decently. Decadence has now made it fashion to expose as much bosom as possible, and no matter how ugly the breasts are, almost every female wants to be part of that fashion. Cameroon is a very small country, so imagine what occurs elsewhere. This is what their God calls sinful temptation of the opposite sex."

"What do the men say about this?" asked Mobuh. "From my knowledge of human men, they prefer what they call cleavage, with just a soupcon of the gorgeous breasts underneath."

"Many of the designers of these sexy attires are men. Besides, most women dress so skimpily to impress them. A few men openly protest against such dressing but deep inside, they secretly take in all that is available for them to see. Actually, men would not enjoy a female artist or performer if she is not sexily dressed."

The screen moved to another scene. Beautiful women of all ages were standing by the road side, smiling invitingly at horny men. Some of the females looked as young as twelve. Yivissi switched over to a war scene where soldiers were busy raping and looting.

"The earth is this decadent?" asked an elderly lady wearing a wig

"Worse!" replied Yivissi. "Their God must be very tolerant. I wonder how he has managed to contain all these things when their book, the Bible, states that he used to punish for a lot less. However, I am sure a little more of this will be the last straw."

"Maybe he is so tolerant because he is now competing with Allah over who shall have more earthlings under him." proposed a sharp-looking middle aged professor. "In their book he was alone and could punish his people in any manner without fear because they had no other super being to turn to. Now, with the presence of Allah, who has already succeeded in having quite a following, God needs to be more careful, otherwise every body will cross over to Allah."

"I read somewhere that Allah is just one of the names by which the human God is known. Allah is supposed to be the same like Yahweh or Jehovah," contributed a short chap.

"That is not true," insisted the middle aged academician. "There are some blokes who call themselves Jehovah's witnesses and they insist that their God is known as Jehovah and nothing else, and most certainly not Allah. The Moslems believe in Allah and that Mohamed is his prophet.The Christians declare that you cannot be saved and go to God without passing through a young fellow they called Jesus, who they claim is the son of God and God at the same time. Some Christians do not believe in the divinity of this Jesus however but still regard him as the only gateway to God. This leaves out the Moslems completely who prefer to pass through their prophet Mohamed, not Jesus."

"With this kind of confusion on who is actually the God of these earthlings, how do you expect that your idea will work?" Mobuh asked, looking at Yivissi

"We have done a thorough study of the whole situation and determined that the earth chaps are fighting over the same God."

"Then how come he gives instructions to one set of believers and something completely contrary to other believers? He has ended up confusing the poor fellows?"

""Like what?" Yivisi was almost getting confused herself.

"Why, don't you see?" asked Mobuh "He allowed pork as a delicacy to some and ordered others not to touch it. He allows Moslems to marry up to four wives, then turns around and declares to Christians that it is sinful to have more than one wife. Look at this situation where this God declares that Jesus is his son and the only gateway into heaven and shortly afterwards brings Mohamed in, declaring to Mohamed's people that Jesus is just a prophet, but Mohamed is greater. Either it is one confused God or the two are different Allah is Allah and Jehovah or Yahweh or what ever name the Christians prefer is their God."

"Well, really sir," protested Yivissi. "You are making things difficult."

"No! I have also conducted my own analysis of the situation."

Mobuh switched on another screen and said: "Watch."

It was some kind of school. An old man with a white beard was lecturing some young fanatics on the virtues of dying for Allah. 'Allah rewards you greatly, he was telling the young men. All you need to do is to blow yourself up with a powerful bomb such that you take down with you, as many infidels as possible. Your reward will be great. When you are blown up, you will land directly into the laps of seventy-two beautiful virgins, all waiting to be yours." Mobuh switched off the scene.

"Such schools are many," he explained. "This old man does not tell these young blighters who will gather their pieces strewn all over the site of the blast before lifting them whole to drop into the waiting arms of the eager virgins. Neither does he bother to explain how Allah, who has decreed that true Moslems are not entitled to more than four wives would supply so many virgins to one young hero alone."

Mobuh took in a deep breath to make his point sink.

"There are many young men lusting for virgins, like the ones we have just seen in the scene, who go blowing up innocent Christians, people of other religions, and even other Moslems. The Christian God has probably decided to leave his own people alone despite the hideous crimes they now commit. How would you then get any of these gods, Allah or Jehovah to destroy his people because of decadence?"

Yivissi, like all the inhabitants of Mungohgoh, had a lot of respect for Mobuh, but he was taking this thing too far.

"With all due respect, sir" she said. "The true Moslems and the true Christian believe in one and the same God. The Old Testament of the Bible of the Christians talks

virtually about the same thing as the Koran of the Moslems.
The Abraham and Isaac mentioned in the Christian Bible is
the same Ibrahim and Isaac in the Koran. What makes this
God docile for now is that they have not touched him on
the worst spot. He is used to all sorts of earthly crimes, and
has learnt to tolerate many things. It is true that when he
just created the world, he was a bit impatient. Many
earthlings don't quite understand him and interpret his
action in various ways. Some claim to know him better than
others"

Yivissi wiped a few drops of perspiration from her face.

"Now look at this one."

Yivissi switched on the screen again.

The scene that came up showed an old bloke, dressed in
one of those flowery African robes, talking bitterly to a
young neighbour dressed in sport gear.

"You seem to have shirked church service again," the
old bloke was telling the young man.

"Yea" replied the young fellow. "I have nothing to ask or
beg from God, neither has he given me any nice thing for
me to go thanking him."

"But you always have to thank God for giving you life,
for keeping you healthy, for giving you food."

"I did not ask him to give me life. Besides, every living
thing is only healthy if it takes care of itself properly, and
has enough food only if it works for it. Why then should I
go thanking God for these things?"

"That is blasphemy. God could punish you for saying
that."

"So, God has become such an irrational being? Why
should he punish me simply for not thanking him for nothing,
whereas the whole world is committing hideous crimes
everyday and going scot-free?"

The old man was livid with anger

"You are a pagan," he shouted. "A devil! Lucifer's own son"

"I do not believe in Lucifer either. In fact I do not even think he exists."

"God will certainly punish you for that."

"Are you saying that God punishes people who do not believe in Lucifer? Anyway, I have all I need and can do without extra comfort. I have achieved through my own sweat. Let those lucky fellows who were born into rich families or those parvenus who have suddenly found themselves wallowing in wealth thank God for what he has given them."

"But are you not grateful that God has given you the intelligence and the capacity to earn a proper living. You should be grateful for your wife and children."

'Even animals that have to be sold or eaten have females to make love with, and equally make children. It is a natural process. You see, all of you fanatics have lost reason completely and foolishly believe in a God without stopping to think. When you are seriously ill and finally get well, your family says that God loves you very much and that is why he saved your life. If on the other hand you die, they say God let you die because he loves you very much, much more than they do."

'That is heresy!" the old bloke shouted, "and unfortunately there are many of you in this world. We should expect another deluge and should not blame God this time."

The scene had been very captivating. All the scientists had concentrated so much on it that there was a general groan of protest as it was suddenly switched off by Yivissi.

"That old fellow is right." Yivissi said firmly. "So many people are challenging the existence of God that with a little push from us they will go overboard and bring down the wrath of God upon them."

"But I am still worried about this God and Allah business. True Moslems are quite straight, and there are many. It is just a small group of them who go shedding blood all over in Allah's name." said Mobuh.

"Maybe," replied Yivissii, "just like there a few true Christians. But then, the bad eggs considerably outnumber the good ones."

After listening thoughtfully to Yivissi's idea, King Awobua dismissed it out right. "The people on earth have reached the peak of decadence and no divine punishment has been vented upon them. Bad people continue doing bad things, live long and comfortable lives, and neither fear nor believe in the existence of any God. On the other hand, good people and small innocent children have miserable lives, mercifully short at times, believing that some day God will change things for the better, and good things never come. The communists were right when they accused Russian priests as dishonest. These men of the cloth lived lavish lives sponsored by the rich nobility, while comforting the peasants that they would easily go to heaven while their rich lords would find it virtually impossible to enter the kingdom of God."

"I think you are right, Sir." said Mobuh.

"Of course, I am right. Life on earth is a dog-eat-dog situation and there is no god to do anything about it. You even wonder why some claim that there is only one God. The Moslems have Allah and worship him in a completely different way from which the Christians worship theirs. The followers of Allah face Mecca and pray. Their prayers are short and concentrated, unlike Christians who spend hours in church, thus giving room for the minds of the worshipers to wander to other frivolous topics. While the Moslems keep repeating that Allah is great and Mohamed is his prophet, the Christians ignore Mohamed completely and concentrate on Jesus. Why, many Christians even claim that this Jesus is God, which makes a third god apart from Allah and God. Then you have the followers of Buddha, who have a Dalai Lama as the reincarnation of the Buddha. This big confusion proves that we can not rely on God to bring destruction to the earth."

Mobuh was quiet.

"This God was never seen by anybody. In all the cases they only claimed to have heard a voice in the wilderness or some such place."

"That is true, Sir," Mobuh was quick to support his king. "Even Moses and Abraham, with whom the Christian God was supposed to have had the most encounters, never saw him."

"That Moses fellow was quite sharp," the king said admiringly. "He built up much from oral tradition to come out with chapters on Abraham, but where he shows that he is a real genius is to have come out with a version of how the world came about, a version which has been accepted as the absolute truth by all Christians."

"It is said that he was inspired, sir. Coming up with such history at a time when science was not quite developed was really a feat."

"Inspired by whom? The chap simply had talent like Shakespeare, and used it well."

13

King Awobua took a few sips from the *mukal* mug he had by his side and remained thoughtful for a while. Then he coughed lightly and pointed at Mobuh.

"We have intelligent scientists with wonderfully sharp brains, you claim?"

King Awobua asked this calmly.

"Yes Sir," replied Mobuh reassuringly.

"And these tough fellows of yours have introduced all types of complicated pestilences and even a super bomb on earth."

"Yes your highness"

King Awobua caressed the chin of a dwarf kneeling by his side.

"And in spite of all this, it is a dwarf who has given me the best solution to conquering the earth?"

Mobuh was taken aback. Dwarfs had been known to be stupid creatures, meant to serve as side stools for the king. Their additional role of serving the king with drinks and bringing him this and that was only introduced when it was decided that as few Mungongoh citizens as possible should have access to the king. Being made to act as punching bags was the only other use to which they could be put. Never had it been considered that a dwarf could be so bold as to talk to the king, let alone suggest a good idea. Ideas were supposed to come from an institute of experts and researchers.

"You are saying that a dwarf had the audacity to talk to you, Sir? I will arrange for his punishment immediately."

"You will arrange for a better status for dwarfs. I have discovered that they are more intelligent than you blokes."

"But Sir, you can't be the king of a bunch of dwarfs."

"I have realized that too" admitted the king. "And that is just the problem. However, let us see what we can make of the situation."

"You mean to say you went consulting dwarfs, Sir?" Mobuh wanted to get things straight.

"Not really." The king rubbed the head of the dwarf whose cheek he had caressed fondly. "This little fellow here had been eavesdropping on everything that transpired here. Somehow he has never been in the way when ever I needed a dwarf to pounce on. It is a good thing though, because he is a smart little chap and what he came up with could be a solution to what all of you smartasses will never deliver."

"May I have the honour of knowing this wonderful idea that came from the lips of a dwarf, Sir?" Mobuh asked carefully.

"His suggestion is simple. He advised that we wage a full scale war with the earth and crush the earthlings."

"But that is not possible, Sir!" Mobuh was aghast.

"Why not?" enquired the king.

"But Sir, the earth is so big and we are just a small rocky satellite of Mars. Where shall we have the resources to crush them?"

"We have certain advantages that will work to our advantage. We are more intelligent than the earthlings, and have succeeded in developing all the things that you blokes have experimented with on earth. We should therefore not underrate our capacity."

"With all due respect Sir, the earth is large and has wonderful defence systems. It is not possible to go on a full scale war with them."

King Awobua banged on the head of the dwarf in anger. As it howled in pain and dropped to the floor, King Awobua turned reproachfully to Mobuh.

"Now look what you've made me do. I almost destroyed a good fellow. No more arguments. Summon those incompetent rascals of yours and make them come up with a plan to conquer the world. I am certain that nothing but out right war will succeed."

Mobuh hurried away to summon Itoff and his gang of tough eggs. He was not sure of how he would handle it, but he had no option.

involving the whole earth at once may lead to an explosion of a scale that could affect us." This was Yivissi's idea.

"What do you propose, then?" asked the excited Funkuin.

"All of us should be given time to think and come up with constructive ideas; we don't have to rush anything," Itoff proposed.

Mobuh realized it was time he stepped in.

"All of us are aware of the fact that up till now we have proposed ideas to our king that have all ended in fiasco. If we had not had such a considerate and forgiving king, all of you would by now have been transformed into lion shit. Our king jumped at this idea from a mere dwarf out of desperation. He has already concluded that he wants full-scale action. Be it a war, or otherwise. Your contributions should consider these aspects."

One of the animal biology professors cleared his throat and said:

"The king is right about a full-scale attack. We have combined different pestilences, using various animals as transmitters, but we have always relied on the earthlings themselves for propagation. But the earthlings have their control measures, vaccines and cures. Maybe if, instead of infecting a few monkeys with Ebola and AIDS, infecting a few rats with the Fire plague, infecting a few birds and pigs with the flu, etc., we had carried out massive production of these pestilences and sent down many of our agents to carry out full-scale infection of all these animals, and even of the earthlings directly, then we would be able to launch a full-scale attack."

Mobuh shook his head. "The idea is good, but think of the costs. Imagine how much *Kuo* we will need for such expensive operations. We will need a considerable number of agents on earth, stealing and sending back materials with which to produce the pestilences. We will then face the next step of our spies moving around the earth and infecting these animals and persons themselves. But with our tiny population, how many spies do you think we can have on earth at any given time?"

"The earthlings are highly corruptible. We could corrupt quite a good number of them to collaborate with our spies." Itoff said.

"That is eminently possible," replied Mobuh.

"Many earthlings are already working with our spies. You are aware of the fact that they are very expensive to run and it is very risky to involve too many of them. Just one of them can turn patriotic at any moment and betray everything."

"Are we now saying that a full-scale operation is completely out of the question?" asked Funkuin.

"Certainly not!" exclaimed Mobuh. "We are here to find out any possible ways of engaging the earthlings in a full scale operation. Let us then try to see what we can combine to come up with a full-scale intervention. We shall use our spies to exaggerate hatred among the earthlings and promote war. At the same time, we shall dispatch many agents to go down to earth and send back as much materials as possible."

"I suggest that they also go for nuclear bomb materials so that we can combine the two," Funkuin added.

"No problem," agreed Mobuh. "Out there, nothing that we can use should be spared."

15

The next month was quite hectic in Mungongoh as agents were trained to penetrate the earth and take back whatever important materials would contribute towards the grandiose plan. The agents were made to master the name 'Innocent' and fully accept it as their name. Their knowledge of the earth was polished, alongside their taste for food and drinks of the earth. With the decision to execute the new plan of a massive attack, the problem of materials had become acute, as Mungongoh scientists were working night and day. To make nuclear bombs for example, it was necessary to have enough plutonium and the other necessary materials. Mungongoh was just a small rocky satellite and was not well endowed. King Awobua's desire to conquer the earth was so hot that caution was thrown to the winds and a large number of agents were now operating on earth.

The act of stealth in theft is important when things have to be smuggled out of high-security areas and transported to special areas where flying saucers are docked. Stealth also requires actions in small doses, not the kind of invasion that was going on. With part of the increased spy staff of Mungongoh involved in sneaking out this or that item from the earth, it was but normal that a few of them would be apprehended in action. The name 'Innocent' was appropriate in this case, but the mistrust between the peoples of the earth presented a more appropriate solution to the Mungongoh agents.

The first agent was caught in America trying to sneak plutonium out of a research labs for defence research. The handsome Mungongoh spy was taken to a panel of interviewers, where he was mistaken for a Russian spy. The smart young man discovered this advantage and acted along, leaving aside the 'Innocent' gag.

"It is the KGB that sent you, right?"

"I don't know the KBG."

"You want to be subjected to torture before you talk? Then why did you need the plutonium?"

"I was sent by my masters."

"Who are your masters then, if they are not the Russians?"

"Do you need to know them?"

"Don't try to be a smartass," said the chief interrogator. "We will fix you alright."

"But I am not Russian. I don't speak the damned language. Neither do I know about Karl Max, Engels and Lenin."

The lie detector proved beyond doubt that he was not Russian. It also proved beyond doubt that he was not a communist.

"Fine," concluded a smart-looking interrogator. "The Russians have discovered another way of penetrating us. They have now employed non-Russians to do their dirty work for them."

His boss was thinking along the same lines.

"Don't play dumb with us," he told the Mungongoh spy sternly. "We know your type. For the pleasure of a few beautiful Russian dames and for the love of money, you are prepared to sell the freedom and democracy which the Western world has achieved through much sweat and blood. What are the Russians paying you?"

The Mungongoh spy remained mute. He could 'admit' that he was working for the Russians as the CIA fellows were insinuating, but that would have made them suspicious. A spy only admits anything when he has no other choice.

"I was going to warm your mother's soup with the plutonium."

The chief investigator lost patience and would have landed the spy a solid slap on the jaw if he had not been restrained by strict American laws.

The fellow under interrogation realised that the American was making a very serious effort to restrain from striking him. It was clear that the interrogator may soon actually lose control of himself.

"If you so much as lay a finger on me, I will send a serious complaint to human rights organizations all over the world" threatened the spy.

"You might as well go and complain in heaven," advised the investigator sarcastically. "I will use any possible method to extract information from you. Don't push me to start imagining the pleasure of actually killing you."

The spy realized that he had to tread carefully. He felt pain like any human and would die if harmed seriously enough. At the same time, the human hangman sitting in front of him looked serious and determined.

"What do you want from me? I have proved that I am not a Russian."

"You don't have to be, greedy pig. You could be an Argentinean for all I care. My problem here is whether you work for them."

"I have said I don't."

"Then where were you smuggling the plutonium to? To Burundi?"

The chief investigator decided to try another trick.

"How much are the Russians paying you for this? Here in America we are richer and more liberal with our spies. We pay several times more than the Russians. May be you would like to spy for us too?"

Underground somewhere in Moscow, specifically at Dzerzhinsky Square, another Mungongoh spy was being led into a special interrogation room. He had been apprehended at Vunukova Airport with a dangerous-looking piece of equipment, apparently trying to send secret messages, as the police concluded.

The experienced KGB major who had been assigned the task of interrogating the dangerous spy was having a preparatory cigarette before indulging in the hideous task of using several ingenuous methods to extract information from the tough-looking infiltrator. They always looked like this when they were brought in, but always broke down into whimpering jerks after an encounter with Major Travinsky. After finishing his cigarette, the major shouted for captain Voloshenyuk to join him. The two Ukrainians made a formidable pair and were so tough that they could make a bishop admit that he had been having an affair with the catechist's wife.

"Now," major Travinsky said in Russian, "You will tell us everything; who sent you, what your mission is, and how you managed to sneak into the Soviet Union. Note that the two of us have a special name among western spies. I am Ivan the terrible, and he is Grozny Hahol." Major Travinsky was now pointing at Voloshenyuk.

He turned again to the Mungongoh fellow.

"Who are you?"

"I am Innocent," the strange agent replied like a recording machine on playback.

"Innocent" repeated Major Travinsky. That name could be American, English, or even French if pronounced rightly.

"And where specifically are you from?" asked Captain Voloshenyuk.

While every tough spy caught in America was considered as definitely Russian, the KGB had several spy networks in the West to deal with. A spy could come from America, Britain, France, or Germany. Spies had even been caught before who were of Chinese or Japanese origin, but working for America. There were even blacks who could easily pass for students of the Patrice Lumumba People's Friendship University at Miklukho Maklaya Street. The Russians really had a more difficult task.

"Where are you from?" repeated Voloshenyuk threateningly.

He shouted for Sergeants Torokanov and Volobuyev to bring in the strange instrument that the agent had been caught with.

"I am from the West" the Mungongoh spy hastened to reply.

"That is no answer. You could still leave the East and come through the West.

"You are from which country?"

"America."

Travinsky observed the agent closely. He was giving in too fast. Either he was not a trained spy or he was from some other country.

"Who are you working for?"

"The CIA, of course."

"What do you think?" Major Tavinsky asked Captain Voloshenyuk, "Is this a normal case? They normally resist till you have almost tortured them to death."

Before Captain Voloshenyuk could say anything, the man under interrogation jumped in:

"There is no use denying that I am a CIA agent. You would still find out after applying your horrible torture methods on me."

"That is true," grumbled Voloshenyuk who had already prepared himself to have a field day.

"What is this instrument and what did the CIA send you here for?" Voloshenyuk was hoping that the foreign agent would hesitate to talk this time and give him the chance to upgrade his torture skills.

"This is a simple communication system. I was simply calling my boss to tell him my position."

"And you had come from where? What were you doing in Moscow?"

"I only sneaked in to test this communication device," said the Mungongoh agent, trying to look as convincing as possible.

"I am sure you need a few doses of my special recipe for repulsive spies like you. No more blabbing. Why would you want to test a toy like this in enemy territory? You could have gone to Zaire or some other easier place."

"The problem is not distance. The problem is to ascertain whether messages can be sent out without being detected," the Mungongoh spy lied in what he hoped would pass for sincerity.

"But you could have tracked and tested the gadget in America," pointed out Travinsky.

"One never knows. After completing tests in America, it was discovered that Moscow might have some new detecting devices that we were not aware of. That is why I was sent on this special mission."

Major Travinsky turned to Tarokonov and Volobuyev. "Where is Tarielkin? I want a thorough check and analysis of this instrument and its functions. Meanwhile, lock up this son of a bitch." He then turned to Voloshenyuk. "Let us adjourn till tomorrow."

A few more Mungongoh agents were caught in Russia and America. Dangerous laboratory chemicals and materials disappeared from other parts of the world without trace. Constant interrogations by experienced hangmen in Russia and America uncovered a few aspects which pointed to the fact they both had a common enemy. Who it was, they could not tell. Cooperation was thus necessary.

A summit was therefore programmed to take place in Equatorial Guinea, where the big powers including America, the Soviet Union, Germany, Britain, France, Japan, Canada

126

and China were supposed to participate at the highest level. The presidents of these countries were supposed to agree on a common approach to the resolution of this issue and combine their efforts to save the earth from whatever impending doom was looming.

In Mungongoh, news of the apprehended spies was making the rounds, but the general understanding was that the earthlings were merely accusing each other, without the faintest idea of the origin of it all. All the same, the institute of ideas was being blamed for not having put rescue measures in place.

16

The choice of Equatorial Guinea for the summit was arrived at after a few other countries had been considered. It had been agreed that the summit should take place on neutral grounds, not in Washington, Moscow, Paris or Bon. The big presidents equally decided to combine work with pleasure and thought this African island would be just the ideal place.

The meeting of superpowers had actually been organized by the president of America, who had pumped in a lot of money to refurbish the airport and the hotel where their Excellencies were to lodge. The small airport of Malabo was choked with presidential jet planes. Security was tight and traffic police were positioned all over the town.

The meeting hall had been completely renovated and decorated so as to render it befitting for such august visitors. When all the important personalities had come in and were seated, the president of America took the floor.

"Ladies and gentlemen," he said.

The president of the Soviet Union, who was also the chairman of the communist party, adjusted his earphones so as not to miss any bit of the simultaneous interpretation.

"All of you are welcome to this special summit. Although it is restricted to you, the superpowers, it concerns the whole world. The earth is in grave danger and requires immediate action. My colleague of the Soviet Union is more conversant with the problem than you all. You will equally notice among us, the president of Ghana, one of the rare examples of democracy in Africa. You will also find the presidents of India and Brazil, giants to reckon with although they are not superpowers."

He turned to a handsome lady sitting expectantly near him.

"I will now call on my secretary of state to give your Excellencies a picture of what I am talking about."

"Excellencies…" the secretary of state addressed the politicians with all the respect possible. She was aware of the fact that in terms of actual competency and knowledge about managing a country, most of them would be scored below the average mark. However, they were a bit better than many African presidents, who have transformed themselves into monarchs through acquiring the status of presidents for life, despite the mess they have made of their otherwise resourceful countries.

"Excellencies," she repeated by way of getting total attention. "We have all certainly heard about flying saucers although, we may not believe in their existence. Now, we strongly believe that these flying saucers do come in regularly from some heavenly body which we have not yet identified. These flying saucers, we now believe, come in on secrete missions to the earth. It would appear the frequency of their arrival has increased, supporting our view that some terrible plan is in action."

Confused chattering broke out as the different presidents expressed shock in their different languages. Since she was confronting presidents and not naughty school children, the secretary of state was compelled to wait patiently for the commotion to die down.

After an interval, she cleared her throat loudly, a polite way of letting her honourable audience understand it was time they piped down and allowed her to continue.

"For the past three months, we have noticed the mysterious disappearance of certain vital and strategic chemicals and materials from laboratories and elsewhere.

We have even noticed the disappearance of samples of dangerous diseases from research laboratories. Cross checking with other countries has revealed that such unexplained disappearances have occurred there too. In addition, we have caught a few persons actually sneaking out some of these things, even plutonium."

She looked guiltily in the direction of the USSR president.

"I am sorry to say, we suspected the Russians. But they too caught some of these thieves and suspected us. In spite of our thorough investigations, we could elicit very little concerning their reasons for stealing the stuff and the intended destination of the stolen materials."

Another commotion broke out, and this time it took the president of the USA himself to bring back calm.

The secretary of state immediately continued.

"One of the latest criminals we caught had actually sneaked out three vials of bird flu virus and anther two of Ebola virus from one of our high security laboratories, and was taking them to who knows where. On interrogation, like most of the others, he ended all his statements by insisting that he was innocent.

Like the others, he had no trace of a Russian accent in his speech. On further analysis, we discovered that all of them were called 'Innocent'.

"You should add that 'Innocent' is not a Russian name", suggested the Soviet Union president humorously.

There was laughter from all parts as the joke was simultaneously interpreted into the earphones of the participants.

"I beg your permission to continue," the very competent secretary of state said, smiling.

"Go on," encouraged her boss.

"After a lot of hard work we uncovered the fact that the word 'Innocent', used as their names, was meant to derail our lie detectors."

"*C'est formidable!*" exclaimed the French president.

"Yes, who ever employed these agents and trained them was quite smart. We therefore reprogrammed our lie detectors to ignore the word 'Innocent' and passed all the prisoners apprehended through it. From clever questioning and an eventual analysis of all the answers, we deduced that these agents had all come from a strange place called Mungongoh, but where it is, we could not make out."

The Soviet Union president swore in very rapid, complicated Russian, but because of the obscene nature of his words and because it was simply a side comment, the interpreters did not interpret them.

A handful of those strange agents had been apprehended in his country and things had equally disappeared mysteriously, but his country had not analysed the situation up to this stage. It was really shocking to hear that apart from the troubles his country already faced in coping with the obligation of coexisting with decadent capitalist America, another force from outer space might also become a threat.

The Secretary of State continued despite the rude interruption.

"A few other agents apprehended were, beyond doubt, Americans. From every indication, these alien infiltrators from Mungongoh had succeeded in recruiting some of our citizens to do their dirty work for them. From the nuggets of information we extracted, we managed to collate some information concerning their mission on earth. It is quite alarming. The king of this Mungongoh, it would seem, has the great ambition of taking over this earth. But their king is not interested in us humans. He is more intent on wiping us all out of the earth and filling the earth with his own people. He would then make use of our resources. It would appear that several attempts had been made before, but with very limited impact. This time, it looks like a full-scale offensive is being launched and all what is being taken away will be used for this massive offensive."

132

"You did not work out the nature of the offensive?" the prime minister of Britain asked, worried. "We need to know what this offensive is all about and when they plan to launch it."

"I think it would also be important to find out at any cost where this Mungongoh is. The only solution might be a blitzkrieg. Strike the planet with full force and knock it off the solar system before he clears us off the earth," the German chancellor proposed.

"What makes you think that this Mungongoh is within the solar system?" asked the Soviet president. "It could be a satellite of another star within the Milky Way or even in some other galaxy."

"Let the secretary of state continue. We can discuss this later," advised the US president

"Thank you sir," she said "We have no idea where this Mungongoh could be. Neither can we imagine what this serious strike they are brewing could be. We are still working on the bunch of 'Innocents' we have in our custody though, but it would seem that their role was just to steal and take back to this strange planet, or whatever it is, the items that had been listed for them."

"Is it not possible to force the chaps you have captured to direct us to this place, Mungongoh?" the chairman of the People's Republic of China, who had been silent and thoughtful all the while, enquired.

"We have tried that too, but it would seem that their system of transportation is so well organized that only the pilots know where they are coming from and going to.

"We need to get hold of one of the pilots, then," the French president said emphatically.

"It is not that easy, sir," replied the secretary of state. "When the Mungongoh agents operate, they are guided by some force to the aerodrome. The Mungongoh pilots have a very sensitive monitoring system and can easily sense danger from a distance. From every indication every agent that we have apprehended has been cut off from their system somehow."

"So what do we do then?" asked the British prime minister.

"That is why I summoned this meeting," replied the commander-in-chief of America.

"We are all here to be fully briefed on the looming danger so that we can jointly think of something. Our work is actually to lay some foundation and hand over to my secretary of state, who will work with the experts that I asked you to bring along to suggest to us the way forward. You are all aware of the urgency of the matter and I am sure you would understand that we need to spare no cost in order to find a solution. The floor is now open."

The president of Ghana decided to take the lead.

"If we follow the secretary of state's exposé closely, we will see that these intruders have a human form and speak like us. It means that either these strange people who covet the earth so much are quite close to the earth or they have a base on earth, where they get transformed. It also means, I suppose, that these strange beings have been spying on us, coming and going for a very long time. I propose we work those blighters in custody into revealing this base. After all, they have certainly been abandoned and have virtually become humans now."

"Horosho!" shouted the soviet president, who felt he had a sense of humour. "Congrats! When you decided to speak, I feared you were about to propose that we contact a few African witch doctors. I hear they can even succeed in striking enemies with African thunder bolts."

"If Russians spend all of their time joking, in Ghana, we know when to be serious and when to joke," replied the Ghanaian President sternly.

"Really, comrade!" admonished the French president. "Since you never had colonies, you never learnt that you should never be so blunt with our comrades in the Third World. You should learn from us, the French."

"Eh?" the Russian asked.

"Yes" replied the descendant of Louis. "You heap praises on naïve African presidents before twisting their arms to get what you want."

"No wonder former French colonies often have the wrong person as president" said the Ghanaian. "You impose stooges whose arms you can easily twist, and ruthlessly pillage the little that is left over from colonial plunder."

The US president finally stepped in.

"No more bickering," he said. "We are here to discuss serious issues."

"I thing the Ghanaian president has suggested the right thing" said the British prime minister. Let us leave everything in the hands of the secretary of state and her team, who will work on what the president of Ghana has proposed."

"Is my Russian comrade OK with the suggestion?" asked the US President.

"I am all for it, or perhaps you want to see me clapping?"

"Well then, let's call it a day. Malabo has good food, wonderful wine and beautiful women. Enjoy yourselves while our experts work. We will resume when they are through."

17

Back in Mungongoh, King Awobua had summoned Mobuh to his inner sanctum so that they watch the summit of presidents of the super powers.

"At least the advantage we have over them is that we know where they are and we can watch whatever they are doing," Mobuh said comfortingly to the king. "I have gathered all the members of IRDI in their conference room where they are all watching this summit. I have planned very serious discussions with them at the end of all this."

"I hope from their discussions you fellows will be able to surface with the absolute idea. The blockheads on earth will be talking freely, not suspecting that they are being closely monitored," said King Awobua.

The king was very quiet during the exchanges between presidents.

"Have you noticed that there is virtually no woman among these politicians?" he finally observed.

"Female earthlings have always had to fight very had in order to place themselves anywhere important sir. The woman you see presiding is very intelligent and competent. That is what has propelled her to that position." Mobuh replied

"Anyway, they don't seem to be heading anywhere," said King Awobua smugly. "It is a pity that quite a number of our agents have been apprehended."

"Let me go and assess the situation more thoroughly with my academicians" Mobuh proposed. "I will be back sir."

As Mobuh strode importantly into the hall, everybody stood up in respect and waited until he ordered them to sit.

"I suppose you have all watched the meeting that just took place on earth. These are the main decision makers and everything they say is final. Right now their technicians are working to come out with something for them to endorse. From every indication, they won't come out with much. Now let's hear from all of you. What do you think?"

"We could blow up all those tough guys in the summit," proposed Funkuin. Our small nuclear bomb here has enough power to blow up the whole damn island where they are meeting."

"And what would we gain from that?" asked Itoff.

"Don't forget that the earth is always on the brink of war. We could make it look like either America or USSR is involved in the terrorist act. War will break out, I assure you."

"What a stupid idea!" shouted Fulumfuchong. All the super presidents are present on this island. Any bomb explosion would kill all of them. The death of all the super presidents together will instead strengthen the solidarity between them.

"I didn't think of that."

"Look before you leap," advised Fulumfuchong. "Always think."

"Yes, Doctor Kinj" said Mobuh to a man who seemed to be itching to say something.

"We have made several attempts to exterminate the earth's population and failed. Through our attempts and failures we have discovered that the earthlings are much tougher than we had expected. Now, from the summit they have just held, we have seen that many of our agents operating on earth have been apprehended. We can make out from their statements that those men are thinking of fighting back, and what is probably holding them back is the fact that they have no idea about where we are located."

138

"And they will never find out," said Yivissi.

"You can't be too sure," said Itoff". You are certainly aware of the fact that they have landed on their satellite called Moon. They have even succeeded in sending their craft to our mother planet Mars. We are simply lucky that they have been concentrating on Mars and are not bothered with a small rocky satellite like ours.

"Itoff is right," said Mobuh. "The earthlings are certainly aware of the existence of Mungongoh. It is just that they don't know the name. And neither do they suspect that it could be inhabited".

"But that is terrible," said Yivissi. "It means that someday they might get tired of their empty moon and the lifeless Mars and transfer their attention to our Mungongoh.

"That is very unlikely," said Itoff. The earthlings will always be interested only in the big planets. You can see that after one or two attempts to get to their moon, they lost interest but have always been attracted to Mars and even more distant planets. Rest assured that we would never be of any interest to them."

"What I was driving at, however," said Doctor Kini, who had been struggling to take back the floor "is that if we are not careful those bloodhounds on earth will trace us and destroy us."

"Explain," said Mobuh.

"I am saying that anybody who watched the summit closely would have deduced that the earthlings now have more information than we would have wished them to have, and this is all due to the considerable number of our agents they have had the possibility of questioning. What I propose therefore is that we suspend everything."

There was a murmur all around until Mobuh stepped in.

"Suspend everything you say, but why? "

"It is easy to see that the situation is getting dangerous. Let's allow things to cool off for a while. When no more dangerous chemicals and materials are stolen, and when no other Mungongoh agents are apprehended, the earthlings will believe that it was some false alarm and relapse into their usual blissful oblivion."

"Have you considered the fact that the king's greatest ambition is to crush these blighters as soon as possible?"

Mobuh was almost foaming at the mouth.

Doctor Kini remained calm. "We are also talking about the safety of Mungongoh. The king will no doubt preside over the earth someday, but from every indication it will not be soon. For now I believe our priority is to save Mungongoh. Stop anymore trips down to earth; suspend even the Institute of Ideas from thinking for a while."

"That is very audacious," said a shocked professor Itoff.

"That courageous Doctor Kini is quite right," King Awobua said when Mobuh reported the contents of the meeting to him, fearing the worst.

"Arrange for all links with those agents who have been apprehended to be permanently severed. No attempts should be made to save any of them. All our safe apartments on earth should be closed. Until I say otherwise, we will have no physical contact with the earth."

18

While the experts were poring over the situation and racking their brains to develop ways out of the impasse, some of the heads of government and presidents were enjoying themselves thoroughly. The French president was provided with a handful of male prostitutes to satisfy his homosexual tendencies to the fullest. The Chinese delegation had come with everything, from water to pretty girls. The Japanese prime minister had brought along his favourite geisha and was having a swell time. As for the Russian President, he opted for a handful of mixed-race girls, and exhausted the stock of Viagra he had brought along with the cartons of *pshenichnaya* vodka. The leaders had transformed a crisis meeting into a swell jamboree.

Not all the heads of government were having a frolicsome time, however. The elderly German chancellor had come along with his dear wife, a very stern and reserved Christian who even believed that too much fun and laughter was sinful. They read a chapter from the Bible each night and went to bed in their night clothes, each on his or her own side of the large bed. As for the president of America, he was in a fix. He would have loved to loosen up a bit and sample a few local babes, but Americans were too particular about the public behaviour of their president. For a country which registered the most hideous crimes on earth, which had a language full of obscenities, which paraded sex openly, it was ironical that they expected certain values of their presidents and other representatives. One beauty queen was even deposed because it was discovered that she had once taken a few pictures in the nude. When it concerned their president, the Americans fuss over things that would considered as normal in other countries. After one lonely night, the president was tempted the next night to call the secretary of state to his room as if it were state duty and take potluck, but gave up the idea since he was not sure how she would take it. After all, she was the wife of an important businessman and very powerful.

19

After three days of hard work, the experts finally came up with what they thought would be satisfactory to their bosses. The heads of state were all present, most of them beaming satisfactorily because of the wonderful time they had been having. They were welcomed by the president of the USA who, after a brief speech, handed over to his secretary of state. She was dressed in a beautifully cut cream suit and looked quite handsome as she stood on the rostrum and put on her gold rimmed reading glasses. Her musical voice rang out as she addressed the top men in the world.

"Your excellencies, welcome back to the extraordinary crisis summit of Malabo. I hope you had a swell time while we the experts were working on the problem that is facing the earth currently. We have come up with a few analyses and assessments from which we have certain proposals to present to this august assembly. We hope you will be satisfied with our work."

There was thunderous clapping from the high level audience.

"Thank you," chirped the super star secretary of state. "My colleagues and I are very happy that you are appreciating our work. Thank you very much." She looked at her president for inspiration and continued.

"We all came to the conclusion that we are dealing with a formidable enemy. The enemy knows much about us and we know little about her,"

She used the word 'her' as if she were challenging the men or probing to see whether they would protest on the prominent use of the feminine.

"We discovered that these aliens have been everywhere and in any country where they could find anything valuable to take. The main items that they steal are samples of very virulent diseases which are kept in laboratories for purposes of research, geared towards the development of vaccines, curative drugs or more effective drug options. But we are certain that these people have no intention of developing effective vaccines and cures for these pestilences to hand to us. Rather, we are certain that the stolen samples are meant to be used against us."

The secretary of state paused and appreciated the awed reaction of her honourable audience.

"Apart from pilfering these items that they can use to bring doomsday to our threshold, they have also been helping themselves to plutonium and other materials that we use for making nuclear bombs and warheads. This brings in a bit of confusion. We are now not quite certain whether they plan to eliminate us by blowing up the world sky-high or by using deadly diseases. However, we all agree that the amounts they have succeeded in smuggling out of the earth are considerable, but not yet enough to put mankind out of existence completely."

The audience moved uneasily in their comfortable seats

"Again," continued the Secretary of State "we have assessed that they don't have much else to use against us and that is why they had to rely on these things smuggled out of the earth to wage a successful war. Finally, we believe that a full-scale war with these alien aggressors would be difficult. We know nothing about them, but they apparently know much about us. We must therefore do everything to prevent that war. The first thing is to put a hold on any attempts to smuggle out materials. To ensure this, all laboratories all over the world should be equipped with efficient security systems and guarded full time. All nuclear laboratories, factories and storage areas should be well guarded. We should then place observatories on strategic points on the earth and keep full time watch. We should then place the whole world under a state of emergency. All the superpowers here present will create a team of bloodhounds that will move round and sniff out any bases or ports where their flying saucers, or whatever craft they were using, docked to collect cargoes of the dangerous material that had been stolen from the earth. We need to capture just one spacecraft for our scientists to work on, or one pilot from whom we could squeeze out information about the location of this enemy planet. This, in a nutshell, is the synthesis of our deliberations. Detailed reports shall be taken back by each delegation."

She bowed to the bewildered top fellows and stepped down.

In Mungongoh, the king had been glued to the large monitor in his chambers. Mobuh had been sitting by his side, maintaining a respectful silence. He would have preferred to be out in the meeting hall in the Institute of Research and Development of Ideas, where he would have been most important, but the king had compelled him to remain by his side for this very important event.

"Well, what do you think?" the king asked

"We still have the advantage in that we can watch their every action and eavesdrop on all their planning sessions." replied Mobuh.

"That does not help us much," said the king

"They are right in that we don't yet have enough materials for my full-scale war. Meanwhile we have suspended all action on earth, and that is good too."

"Yes Sir. From every indication, they will toughen things up, and we don't want any of our crafts or pilots falling into their hands," said Mobuh.

The king frowned at the monitor where the American president was now talking to his peers, swivelled round and declared:

"This is my royal decree concerning this situation. Drop everything concerning the earth. Let's give a break of about 15 years. Let them forget completely that anything like this ever happened. Then, we will strike. Our strike shall be devastating."

"But sir, how shall we get the materials with which to develop the capacity that will enable us to deliver a well packed punch on those earthlings?"

"Simple, my dear boy," replied the king, sounding like Sherlock Holmes talking to Dr Watson.

"We shall do absolutely nothing for the first ten years. During the following five years, however, we shall start sneaking in our agents in search of the materials. This time however, it will not be on such a massive scale and the earthlings will never suspect anything. Even if a few of our agents are caught in the act, the foolish earthlings will simply accuse one another."

"That is brilliant!" said the chunky Mobuh. "You are better than all the chaps of the IRDI put together."

"Of course!" replied the elated king. "Who in this kingdom can claim to be brighter than the king?"

"That strategy of yours is the final thing. In ten years, the earthlings will have tired of the expensive and exhaustive measures that they are now planning to implement and will have relaxed everything. They would even have forgotten that at one point they had been close to being destroyed by an unknown enemy."

"You have got it right," said the king. "The earthlings have a greedy nature and are always fighting for power or wealth. They can never unite against us. Even if they attempt to, some hothead like Genghis Khan, Attila or Hitler will surface and bring down everything.

On earth, specifically in Malabo, the president of America finished his brief appraisal of the report of his secretary of state. The floor was now open for the other presidents to speak. The interpreters were very alert.

"Let us applaud the good work done by the secretary of state and her team" proposed the Chinese president. They were used to clapping much during official functions in China. Everybody clapped heartily as the pretty woman beamed appreciatively.

The next speaker was the German.

"I thought our experts would have proposed a massive rearmament program. Those barbarians out there might already have enough weapons and are poised to strike. How do we defend ourselves if we don't have fighting power?"

The efficient secretary of state jumped up.

"Your Excellency, the tendency in the world today is to reduce the production of arms considerably. We have to avoid encouraging arms production in every way, especially nuclear and chemical material. Besides, we are not even sure of the type of arms needed against an enemy that we know nothing about. If in the end there is a massive build up of nuclear arms, and no enemy to use it against, then we will be tempted to use it against one another on the slightest provocation."

"What of the option of African witch doctors and thunderbolts," joked the soviet chief, looking mischievously at the Ghanaian president.

The Russian had had a glass of vodka too much during lunch and needed to be restrained.

"We don't have time for jokes right now," the president of the USA said sternly.

The Ghanaian president ignored the prankish statement with distain. The other big men were shocked but silent.

"May I say something?" This time it was the president of Equatorial Guinea. The American president who served as chair person nodded in acquiescence.

"In my humble capacity as president of Equatorial Guinea, I understand that I would not have qualified to sit in this meeting if it were not holding in my country. However since I am here with you, I have my own small opinion, which I hope will be considered despite its humble source."

"Speak on" encouraged the French president.

"The whole world has totally forgotten about God and has completely fallen into sin. Wars of conquest, wars of revenge and destruction of all types are the order of the day. While much of the world is living in sickness, abject poverty and squalor, trillions of dollars are spent on destructive and useless arms. While Russia and America are busy challenging each other, innocent children and citizens of poor Third World countries are suffering. When America discovered the folly of fighting a wasteful war in Vietnam after trying hard to impose a system the people had rejected, the Russians took over and invested heavily in another wasteful war in Afghanistan. Through hatred for one another we have forgotten the words 'cooperation, forgiveness, understanding, generosity and consideration'. We have pushed the whole situation to the wall. Finally, God has sent a signal. If you don't see it, I do. It is clearly written on the wall. God has sent a stranger, an alien, a force that is a threat to all of us, American, Russian, Kenyan, Tajik, Turk or Chukchi, all of us. No body will be spared if they strike. This clearly shows that we should forget about all our differences and come together to defend the earth. After this we must continue to defend the earth together. We cannot succeed in doing this if we continue with greed, covetous attitudes, crime and lawlessness, and disdain for Godly things. My brothers, let us unite."

Everybody seemed to be taken aback by the oratory. Even the Soviet president who considered God and religion as the opiate of the people, was touched. When the US president asked for any further interventions, none was forthcoming. Finally, the British prime minister said conclusively

"The president of Equatorial Guinea has said it all. I am sure we have nothing else to do but forget our differences and unite."

"That is easy to say," commented the Japanese top official "but you don't face any menace from Korean neighbours bent on developing the most powerful nuclear weapons."

"Yeah." croaked the French president whose husky voice was reputed to have been derived from heavy drinking of cognac. "Or an Iranian neighbour that thinks it should have a bigger nuclear arsenal than France."

The Japanese prime minister jumped in again.

"I propose that we start by banning all nuclear weapons, rid the world completely of them"

"That is not very possible right now." replied the US president. "However, America and the Soviet Union will start by shelving all nuclear programs. Then we will turn round and enforce the ban. Any country that stubbornly goes ahead will have to deal with the two of us. If we had been working together with the Soviet Union all this while on such issues, the world would not have gotten into this mess that the president of Equatorial Guinea has described so well. We generously provided money and weapons to the Mujaheddin of Afghanistan, just because we hated the Russians so much. We have created and protected monsters in developing countries who have wrecked havoc in these countries, and we did these ugly things just because we did not want to get the slightest whiff of Soviet Russia around any president. Why? America would have benefited a lot more from true friendship and collaboration with Cuba, but because of Cuba's relationship with the Soviet Union, our relationship with Cuba has been very strained. Terrorism has bloomed all over the world because of discord between America and Soviet Russia. All that must stop. You will all agree with me that if the two of us support a course, no culprit will hide behind America or Russia. I hope my Russian comrade is with me."

"*Konyechna*," the Russian answered, jumping up. "If America has finally realized that we are not the devil, and that we could work together to bring peace to the world, then we are moving into a new age. North Korea, Iran, and Hugo, beware!"

He had spoken in rapid Russian and the interpreter was still struggling to convey the message when he sat down smiling from ear to ear.

The president of America got up and strode over to him.

"Let's shake hands."

As the Russian got up and stretched out a huge paw, the American spoke again.

"No, a bear hug will be better."

After a hearty embrace, there was a round of applause and all the big world leaders embraced each other warmly.

Titles by *Langaa* RPCIG